ONE
HALF
OF
THE
SKY

ONE HALF OF THE SKY

STORIES FROM CONTEMPORARY
WOMEN WRITERS
OF CHINA

TRANSLATED
BY
**R.A. ROBERTS
AND ANGELA KNOX**

WITH AN INTRODUCTION BY
FRANCES WOOD

DODD, MEAD AND COMPANY · NEW YORK

These eight stories have been chosen from
A Selection of Works of Contemporary Women Writers,
published by Huacheng Publishing House, Guangdong, China.

Translations © 1987 by William Heinemann Ltd

Published by Dodd, Mead & Company, Inc.
71 Fifth Avenue, New York, N.Y. 10003
Manufactured in the United States of America
Translation originally published in 1987
by William Heinemann Ltd, Great Britain
First published in the United States in 1988
First Edition

1   2   3   4   5   6   7   8   9   10

Library of Congress Cataloging-in-Publication Data
Tang tai nü tso chia tso p'in hsüan. English.
Selections.
One half of the sky.

Selected translation of: Tang tai nü tso chia tso
p'in hsüan.
Bibliography: p.
1. Chinese fiction—Women authors
    — Translations into English.
2. Chinese fiction—20th century
    — Translations into English.
3. English fiction—20th century
    — Translations from Chinese.
I. Roberts, R. A. II. Knox, Angela. III. Title.

PL2515.T362513   1988   895.1'3'01089287   87-24646
ISBN 0-396-09291-8

CONTENTS

INTRODUCTION

FRANCES WOOD

LIKE MANY OTHER cultures, China has no tradition of women's literature. Like the women of many other cultures, those of China were confined to the home, forbidden to leave the confines of the courtyard, their view of life as restricted as that of a 'frog in a well'. Glimpses of the outside world through the front gate or over a garden wall, an annual New Year trip into the streets in curtained sedan chairs, were all there was for well-brought-up women. One man, laying down the rules for proper behaviour within the clan or extended family in the seventeenth century, even suggested that corridors and galleries should be designated for use only by men or by women, to avoid unseemly meetings within the home.

At the beginning of the twentieth century, the outside world had imposed itself on China and the traditions of centuries began to be questioned. Young men cut off their pigtails, partly as a gesture of defiance against the crumbling Manchu ruling house, partly because short hair was more 'modern'. For women, change was more difficult. Though education gradually became more of a possibility, no other career than marriage was socially acceptable. It was the plight of women that moved Mao Zedong to write his first published articles in 1919. Appalled by the suicide of a local bride who had cut her throat in the bridal sedan chair rather than marry a man she hardly knew but heartily disliked, Mao condemned the social climate that left her no respectable alternative.

Impetus was added to a slowly growing women's movement by the anti-Japanese demonstration on 4 May 1919, which grew into a patriotic self-strengthening movement rooted in the new universities and schools. Begun in protest against Japan's demands to take over the old German 'concessions' in China at the end of the First World War, the May 4th Movement turned into a literary reform, abandoning the almost incomprehensible classical prose that was the property of the bureaucratic élite for new literature written in the vernacular, accessible to all. For some who almost depaired of transforming China, literature was the only way: the great writer Lu Xun (1881–1936) abandoned medicine, where he could only deal with one patient at a time, for literature, whereby he could touch thousands.

The older generation, indeed the first generation, of women writers, represented here by Ding Ling and Bing Xin, grew up at this time and, like their fellow students, threw themselves into the May 4th Movement. They were both unusual in that they came from families that encouraged their education; the opposite of the suicidal bride's. Ding Ling's mother, widowed young, became a teacher in defiance of the traditional view that a widow's life was over with the death of her husband. She supported her impetuous daughter as she broke further new ground, risking her life in political activity, braving society by living in a ménage-à-trois in Shanghai and beginning to write stories about Shanghai characters: left-wing idealists and pampered women.

Though tough in her attitudes and fierce in her views, Ding Ling's fiction shows some of the faults noted by Gladys Yang, the foremost translator in China: 'immaturity, lack of sophistication and verbosity' [Introduction to *Seven Contemporary Women Writers*, Peking, Panda Books, 1982]. For Ding Ling and Bing Xin, the short story in the vernacular was a new form, a product of the movement towards the vernacular and of translations. The short story had flourished in the seventh and eighth centuries but written in classical language; expressions of emotion existed in Chinese literature but expressed, often with subtle indirectness, in the same classical language. The vernacular was a new language without the constraints of tradition; Bing Xin translated Tagore, amongst others, part of the wave of literature from the outside world that was there for exploration, ingestion or incorporation in the search for new forms.

For the younger generation of writers, Xu Naijian, Zhang Xinxin and Zhang Kangkang, the Cultural Revolution of 1966–76, which broke out just as they reached their formative years, meant that they were cut off from the outside world and its literary influences, which were seen as invariably corrupting. Though many critics try to find evidence of external influence in their writing, they frequently explain that they have only been able to read Western works in the last few years, after they had started writing. They are now beginning to experiment with new forms and ideas, breaking through the long-imposed restrictions which tied writers for so long.

Middle-aged writers like Ding Ning, Yu Ru and Ru Zhijuan were most strongly subject to political guidance, particularly after Mao Zedong had laid the ground rules in his *Talks on literature and art* in 1942. With his characteristic directness, he stated that Lenin had solved the question of an audience: literature and art should serve the masses (and not petty-bourgeois intellectuals). Similarly, they should come from the masses: creative workers were to study the lives of peasants and workers and create upon that basis, 'portraying and educating the masses'.

The subject matter of women's fiction is immensely varied; their work is perhaps characterised by a refusal to automatically write 'as women'. It is not uncommon for them to choose a man as narrator, perhaps to deflect easy interpretation. One of Bing Xin's early works was called *About Women*, a first-person narrative in which the narrator was a man; it is a very amusing lightly satirical piece, very different from her sensitive (some would say over-sensitive) stories and poems. Yet problems specific to women, the exploitation of professional women, the near-impossibility of reconciling the demands of home and work and the double standard, expecting virtue from women and accepting less from men, preoccupy the group of middle-aged women writers.

Younger writers who, because they are of a later generation, seem to feel some of these constraints less strongly, have written of the horrors of the Cultural Revolution when they grew up amidst common brutality, but they also write more personally, dealing with the socially smaller, but personally more important, aspects of love and marriage. Though some of their preoccupations (like the social need to be married) may seem strange to western readers, though some of the emotions are over-heightened, as in Ding Ling's work, if you read between the lines, they inform. As so little is still known about China today, particularly the feelings of the Chinese, fiction is perhaps the only medium of information.

The stories in this collection, taken from a three-volume compendium first published in Guangzhou (by Hua cheng chu ban she 1980), have been chosen to illustrate the range of women's fiction in twentieth-century China and to offer stories which have not been widely available in translation before. Biographies are appended, with a list of other translations of women's fiction.

ONE HALF OF THE SKY

LONELINESS

BING XIN

XIAOXIAO SAT IN the classroom labouring through a Chinese exam. His mind was fully occupied with other things, so he hastily dashed off a few sentences and handed in his paper. As he passed it in, the teacher raised his head and looked at him. 'Have another look at it and see if you've written any character wrong. Classes haven't finished yet. What's the rush?' He had no choice but to go back to his seat and fix his eyes on the exam paper, but he sat there blankly, lost in thought.

Finally school was let out, and Zhao Mama came to meet him. As soon as he saw her, he asked, 'Have Aunt and Little Sister arrived yet?' Zhao Mama smiled. 'Yes, you'd better hurry home. Your sister is a lovely little girl.' Hearing her reply, he ran on ahead, and though she repeatedly called to him to wait, he just pretended he hadn't heard.

Running up the steps into the house, he heard his mother call him from inside the room, 'Xiaoxiao, quickly! Come and see your aunt.' He pushed aside the bamboo door-screen and saw his mother sitting with a young woman. He rushed forward and bowed, and the young woman hugged him. She did not speak, but the tears poured down her cheeks. Mother said, 'Let your aunt rest for a while. Go out and play with your sister – she's looking at the fish in the back courtyard.' Xiaoxiao went out, and following the verandah around the house, saw Sister in a light blue tunic, black hair tied in a long ponytail with a wide, light-blue satin ribbon, talking with Zhao Mama next to the fish tank.

Zhao Mama gave her a push. 'Your brother's come.' Sister turned her head and looked at him, then grasped Zhao Mama's hand and giggled. Zhao Mama spoke to him. 'Xiaoxiao, you two play together. I've got other things to do.' Xiaoxiao went over to the fish tank and Zhao Mama left.

Xiaoxiao said, 'Sister, see what you think of my fish. I caught them all in the stream out the back.' Sister just looked at him and laughed. Seeing that she was not going to answer, he also leaned over the side of the tank to watch the fish, and neither of them spoke again.

At the evening meal, Mother, Aunt and the two children chatted to each other affectionately, and he and Sister gradually got to know each other. After dinner Mother and Aunt went on to the verandah outside to enjoy the cool breeze, but Xiaoxiao and Sister stayed inside playing. Xiaoxiao brought out a lot of toys, and they played together under the light of the lamp. Xiaoxiao talked most – chatting about this and remarking on that, while Sister just laughed and looked at him.

Mother called to them from outside, 'Don't be late to bed, tomorrow. . .' Xiaoxiao answered quickly, 'Don't worry, I've already finished my exams, so tomorrow's a holiday. I don't have to go to school.' But Sister was feeling tired, and of her own accord, got down from her chair to go to bed. Xiaoxiao had no choice but to go back inside and get into bed. But he thought that, as soon as it was light tomorrow morning, he and Sister could go fishing.

He got up very early, but Zhao Mama wouldn't allow him to wake Sister, so he had to play by himself in the courtyard. Some time later he heard Aunt and Mother talking indoors and could hear that Sister was also up, so he pushed open the door and went in. Sister was standing in front of the bed while Aunt brushed her hair for her. Seeing Xiaoxiao come in Aunt said, 'Xiaoxiao really is a good student. He was up so early!' He laughed and went forward to wish her a good morning.

After breakfast the two children wanted to go out. Mother

instructed Xiaoxiao, 'Take good care of Sister. The stream is deep and it would be no joke if she were to fall in. Be careful not to get your clothes wet too!' Xiaoxiao immediately assented and then went out with Sister.

Once through the back door, a clear stream stretched across their path. Weeping willows on the banks cast their fresh, green reflections on the water. The two children walked along picking up stones, then finally sat down on a large rock at the water's edge and began to chat.

Sister said, 'We don't have a stream where we live. When you open the gate, all you see is a road with lots of horses and carts going to and fro. In the evening there are electric lights all along the street. It's much more lively than here, but it's not as nice and cool.' Xiaoxiao said, 'I love lively places, but here it's good for fishing, and there are crabs too. In the summer you can watch the farmers cutting wheat and hauling it away in big carts. On summer evenings Mother and I often sit under the trees here and listen to the running water and the cicadas.' While he was speaking, Xiaoxiao stood up and leapt on to a large rock in the stream.

The rock wobbled a little, and Sister called, 'Be careful! You'll fall in.' Xiaoxiao laughed and said, 'I'm not afraid. I've fallen in plenty of times. Look at the scars on my legs.' He rolled down his socks and pointed to his calves. Sister shook her head and laughed. 'Well, I'm scared, I'm scared of things that rock. Even when I'm on the swing at school, I don't dare to swing too high.' Xiaoxiao said, 'Of course – it's because you're a girl.' Sister objected, 'Not necessarily. My classmates all swing really high. None of them are afraid.' Xiaoxiao laughed. 'So that makes you even more of a scaredy-cat girl.' Sister laughed again, unable to find a reply.

Xiaoxiao gazed all around, then suddenly asked, 'Why did Auntie cry yesterday?' Sister said, 'My brother Xuan died. Didn't you know? If Mother hadn't been so upset, we wouldn't have come here.' Xiaoxiao said, 'My mother wrote to Uncle inviting you and Auntie to come for a few days, I heard – but why did your brother die?' Sister beat the water lightly with a willow twig. 'I don't know what kind of illness it was either. The first few days he was fine and still played with me when he came home from school, but then one evening he lost consciousness and was taken to hospital. He died a few days later. I didn't know until the day when Mother came back from the hospital with swollen, red eyes. Father went and buried him, then came back and locked all of his things away so as not to let Mother see them. One day I was looking for a textbook and pulled them out by accident. Mother cried and I cried for a long time too. . .' Sister was clearly on the verge of tears. Xiaoxiao thrust his hands into his trouser pockets and looked at her fixedly. After a long while he said, 'Don't worry, I'm your brother too.' Sister gave a faint smile and replied, 'But you're not my mother's child, you're not my real brother.' Xiaoxiao could find no reply, so he said, 'That makes no difference, don't be upset. Look at all those dragonflies on the water over there. It's going to rain soon. I'll catch some of them for you to play with.'

As they had expected, it rained that afternoon, so they played in the dining-room. They found several long pieces of fine thread, and tied a dragonfly to each end. When released, the dragonflies flew wildly about the room, but because they were restricted by the random movements of the insect at the other end of the thread, they did not fly very high. Sister stood on a chair clapping her hands and laughing in delight. But suddenly one dragonfly flew into her face, causing its hapless mate to dangle across her sleeve, beating its wings furiously. She began to shout in terror, but Xiaoxiao just watched, roaring with laughter. Only when Sister panicked and jumped down from the chair did he rush forward and disentangle the dragonflies. Sister seemed to be angry, so he tried to coax her back into a good humour, while at the same time he opened the door, broke the threads and released all the dragonflies.

It rained solidly for several days. Unable to go out, Xiaoxiao and Sister sat under the verandah, watching the rain and telling stories. Xiaoxiao had told all the stories he knew, so all he could do was make up one of his own. He thought for a while, then began, 'Once there was an old lady who had two sons. The younger one was called Pigsy, and the older one was called Tu Xing Sun. . .' Sister laughed, 'That's not right. Pigsy didn't have a mother, and his brother wasn't called Tu Xing Sun, he was Brother Monkey. You think I haven't heard *Journey to the West*?' Xiaoxiao laughed too. 'I was talking about another Pigsy, not the one in *Journey to the West*.' Sister shook her head, laughing. 'There's no need to try to cover up, I know you're making it up as you go along.' There was nothing Xiaoxiao could say, so he said, 'OK, then you tell me a story.' Sister thought for a moment, then said, 'Long ago . . . long ago there was a king who had a daughter named Princess Snowflake. The princess was very beautiful. . .' Xiaoxiao interrupted, 'Someone tried to harm her didn't they?' Sister looked at him. 'That's right. If you've already heard it, I won't tell any more.' Xiaoxiao said hastily, 'No, I haven't heard it. I just guessed that's what would happen. Do go on.' Sister continued, 'Later the queen died and the king took a second wife called . . . I've forgotten her name . . . anyway, the new queen saw that Princess Snowflake was more beautiful than her and became angry. She sent her into the wild mountains and told an old lady to persuade her to eat a poisoned apple. . .' Xiaoxiao asked quickly, 'Did someone save her?' Sister laughed. 'Don't rush things – afterwards – I can't remember why – Princess Snowflake didn't die. The king realized that the new queen was bad and threw her out of the palace. He had Snowflake brought back and they lived happily ever after.' Sister stopped speaking, so Xiaoxiao asked, 'And what happened after that?' Sister replied, 'It just went on like that, nothing else happened.'

Xiaoxiao stood up and stretched. 'When I listen to stories, I'm most afraid of reaching the bit where everyone's happy ever after. As soon as everyone's happy, the story finishes. Every time Zhao Mama tells me a story, I know that, when she says he became rich or became an official, the story's almost over. What a bore!' Sister said, 'All stories have to end sometime, there's no story that doesn't end – but stories with sad endings are best. I think about sad stories for days after I've heard them. . .' Xiaoxiao suddenly thought of something and said, 'I've got a story that has no end – there was once a king' – he stretched his arms out in a wide gesture – 'who built a granary bigger than the sky, and filled it with more grain than there is in heaven. One day a flock of sparrows flew by. That flock of sparrows was so big that it blocked out the sun. They saw the granary full of rice, found a tiny crack in the walls and flew in one by one. . .' Sister promptly burst out laughing. 'I know! The first sparrow flew in, took a grain of rice in its beak and flew out again, then the second sparrow flew in, took a grain of rice in its beak and flew out again, and so it goes on and on, doesn't it? I've heard my brother Xuan tell that story.' Xiaoxiao said, 'That's right, the person who made up that story was really smart. It really is a story with no ending.' Sister said, 'I don't believe it. Even more rice than there is in heaven can't be more than hundreds of millions of grains. If you went on telling the story day and night, you'd be bound to be finished in a few years.' Xiaoxiao was about to answer when Mother called to them from inside the house, so he remained silent, and together they went inside.

During the night, the rain poured down even more heavily and now and then thunder rumbled faintly in the distance. Xiaoxiao felt terribly dejected: they hadn't been to the stream behind the house for several days now, they'd exhausted their stock of stories, and there was nothing interesting to do in the house. Despondently turning things over in his mind, he gradually drifted into the world of dreams. He dreamed that he went with Sister into a deep forest where they found a huge lake. A girl in white came towards them from the lakeside. She seemed to be Princess Snowflake. In her hand was a large cage full of sparrows. He was just about to speak to her when there was a flash of light before his eyes and she disappeared.

He opened his eyes and found the room full of sunlight. It was a clear day! Unwilling to believe his eyes, he got up and looked out of the window. The sky was a brilliant blue and little birds called cheerfully from the tree branches. The courtyard was several inches deep in water which the wind blew into thousands of tiny ripples. Elated, he dressed immediately and hurried out, his dream completely forgotten.

Sister sat alone on the verandah, rubbing her eyes and gazing around vacantly. Seeing Xiaoxiao, she smiled. 'Brother, it's a clear day!' Xiaoxiao clapped his hands and laughed. 'That's for sure. Look at the water in the courtyard – I dare to get in it!' Sister laughed and looked at him. He took off his shoes and socks and began to paddle through the water, saying with a laugh, 'It's really cool, it's just that the moss on the bottom makes it very slippery.' He began to run slowly, listening to the water splashing around his feet. Sister went over to the edge of the verandah. 'That looks fun, I'm coming in too.' Xiaoxiao bent down and rolled up his trouser legs. 'Come in if you dare, we can play hopscotch.' Sister laughed and sat down on the verandah, but she had only taken off one sock when Mother came out of the house and saw what they were doing. 'Good God! Xiaoxiao, get out of there! Can't you do anything but lead Sister into all sorts of mischief!' Sister promptly put her sock back on, and Xiaoxiao, still laughing, picked his shoes and socks up from the verandah and ran barefoot to the washroom.

After breakfast Mother suggested that they all go out to cheer themselves up. Aunt was reluctant to go, but she couldn't withstand the urging of Sister and Xiaoxiao and had no choice but to go with them. When they got to the park, Mother and Aunt went into a little shop while Xiaoxiao and Sister raced off to the edge of the pool, to watch the ducks washing themselves, before climbing a small hill. The wooded hillside was lush and moist after the rain, and inside a fence at the back of the hill, they found a profusion of wild jasmine flowers in full blossom that seemed to hang in the air like a delicate, scented cloud. Flowering lotuses covered the pool beneath them, and, at the water's edge, they saw a little boat moored. The two of them held a brief consultation, then decided to go and play on the boat. They were just on their way down when they saw Mother waving and shouting to them from a pavilion at the foot of the hill.

When they reached the pavilion, they saw Aunt sitting listlessly against one of the supporting pillars, traces of tears in her eyes. Sister immediately went over to her and nestled close against her breast. Mother said quietly, 'We'd better go home, Aunt is upset again.' Xiaoxiao could do nothing but murmur his assent and follow them out of the park.

In the carriage, Xiaoxiao asked softly, 'Why is Auntie crying again?' Mother replied, 'Auntie saw me buying a little straw hat for you. She thought it looked nice and decided she'd buy one for Cousin Xuan too. But then she suddenly remembered that Xuan was dead and began to cry again, so we came out of the shop straight away – see how deeply a mother feels for her children.' Mother heaved a sigh, and Xiaoxiao fell silent.

Auntie's carriage in front of them stopped outside the sweet shop and Auntie bought Sister and Xiaoxiao two jars of sweets each. Xiaoxiao thanked his aunt, then bought a bottle of banana oil. Sister asked, 'What are you buying that for?' Xiaoxiao smiled. 'To make ice cream with when we get home.'

Back at the house, Aunt was once more overcome with listlessness, so Sister went with her to take a nap. Xiaoxiao ran around busily by himself, searching out the ice cream bucket and preparing everything for making ice cream the following day.

––––––––

Sister woke at dusk, her face bathed in sweat and complaining of the heat. Mother sent her to have a wash, then helped her to wash her hair. Xiaoxiao brought out a large fan and stood on the verandah fanning her vigorously. Sister pushed the hair back from her face with a laugh. 'Stop fanning me, I'm feeling cold!' Xiaoxiao said, 'Then let's go outside. There's a nice breeze under the trees that will dry you off in no time.' The two children went out and sat down on a couple of tree roots.

In the twilight, a new moon hung on the tips of the willow branches. A green-uniformed postman appeared in the distance and made his way towards them. As soon as Xiaoxiao saw him, he put down his fan and ran to meet him, bringing back two letters. Sister asked immediately, 'Who are the letters from?' Xiaoxiao had a look, then replied, 'One is from Father and the other is probably from Uncle. Wait here, I'll take them in.' He raced indoors.

He was back in a moment. Sister said, 'My father's letter is bound to say that he's coming to take us home.' Xiaoxiao replied, 'I don't know – if you go I'll be sure to write to you. I'll address my letters to "Mr Sister Song", OK?' Sister laughed and said, ' "Sister" isn't my formal name and I hate being called "Mr", I like being called "Miss". When Father writes to me from the south, he always calls me "Miss".' Xiaoxiao said, 'That's OK. What is your formal name?' Sister did not reply.

Xiaoxiao fiddled with the edge of the fan and remarked, 'Father's been in England for over a year now. He writes to us about once a fortnight and sometimes a whole lot of letters arrive at the same time. The addresses are written in foreign words that I don't understand, but Mother says that that's my name written there.' Sister asked, 'Why don't you go to England with Uncle?' Xiaoxiao shook his head. 'If Mother doesn't go, I won't go either. I only love my own country. It has trees and water. I don't love England. All they have there is children with yellow hair and blue eyes!' Sister said, 'Our teacher says we should love other countries too – that seems reasonable to me.' Xiaoxiao retorted, 'If you want to, then go ahead. In any case, I've not no feelings left for other countries.' Sister stroked her hair and said, 'One heart can be divided into many parts – take mine for instance: I love Father, love Mother and love many. . .' Xiaoxiao suddenly pointed to the sky and cried out, 'Sister! Quickly, look!' Sister stopped in mid-sentence and raised her head: a small shooting star with a glowing tail streaked across the sky, heading for the horizon.

The night gradually deepened and they went inside. Moving two low stools and a large chair out into the courtyard, they ate their evening meal outside. Mother stood behind Sister, and, after combing the tangles out of her hair, plaited it into two loose braids for her. Xiaoxiao remarked, 'What a nuisance it is to have long hair! I don't have to do my hair when I get up each morning, and it doesn't take long for me to wash my face either.' Sister said between mouthfuls, 'But Mother says that hair has a kind of soft beauty.' Xiaoxiao nodded his head. 'That's true, but I'm sure I wouldn't look beautiful even if I did have long hair.' Everyone laughed – even Auntie.

Next morning they got up early, and Xiaoxiao busily sent Zhao Mama off to wash the bucket and buy ice and salt for making ice cream. Mother measured out the ingredients for them and they began to churn the ice cream under the trees in the courtyard.

Xiaoxiao kept opening the lid to have a look, saying, 'It must be ready now!' but it was still runny. Sister laughed. 'Don't be so impatient, it still hasn't set, if you keep opening the lid the salt will all fall in.' Xiaoxiao spooned out a little of the mixture and tasted it. 'It's tasteless, I should put some of my sweets in there too.' Sister gave an 'OK', and Xiaoxiao added a good number of his orange sweets along with the entire bottle of banana oil. Having done that, he began to worry that it might be too sweet, so he added some boiled water.

Sister spread open her sticky fingers and wiped the sweat from her brow with her sleeve. 'I'm boiling, I can't do any more.' Xiaoxiao said: 'I'll do it. You sit down and have a rest.'

After churning for some time, Xiaoxiao became tired too. He said, 'It must be ready by now. Let's ladle some out and eat it.' Sister spooned some into a cup and tasted a mouthful, but didn't say a word. Xiaoxiao tasted some too, and immediately asked her, 'Do you like it?' Sister laughed. 'It doesn't taste like the ice cream we usually eat – it's a bit sour and a bit salty.' Xiaoxiao put down his cup and clapped his hands with a laugh. 'What do you mean a bit sour and a bit salty? It tastes awful! Let's forget it. We'll give it to Zhao Mama to eat.'

After a hasty clear-up, Xiaoxiao fanned himself with the front of his jacket and remarked, 'I think catching crabs is more fun. Churning the ice cream has made me hot, the best thing would be for us to go and cool ourselves under the shade of the trees.' Sister fetched the fishing-rod and bait, and they went out of the courtyard. Xiaoxiao said, 'See that big rock in the water under that tree? It would be just right for us to sit on. The water's deep there too, so it's good for fishing. If you're scared I'll help you across.' Sister declared that she was not afraid, then supporting herself with the fishing-rod, began to step cautiously from stone to stone across the water.

The stream was swollen after the rain, and the stones seemed like tiny boats floating on its surface. A gentle breeze rippled the water and rustled through the willow leaves. Cicadas chirruped pleasantly and farmland dotted with villages stretched as far as the eye could see. Sister was in high spirits. 'It's lovely here. I don't want to go home again.' Xiaoxiao said, 'This stone is our country. I'll be the president and you can be a soldier.' Sister objected, 'I can't be a soldier. I can't fire a gun – and the firing sound scares me anyway.' Xiaoxiao replied, 'Well, then, you be president and I'll be a soldier – later on this stone will float down the stream to the sea and make another world.' Sister was apprehensive. 'That's no good. I need Mother to do my hair for me.' Xiaoxiao said, 'It doesn't matter if you can't do your own hair, you can just cut it off the same as mine.' Sister said, 'It's not only for doing my hair. I can't do without Mother in another world. If Mother's not there then it doesn't make another world.' Xiaoxiao said, 'I'd like Mother along too, but there's not enough room on this rock.' Sister stood up and pointed with the fishing-rod. 'We could move that rock over here too. . .'

In her excitement, Sister forgot that the rain had made the mossy rock treacherously slippery. She lost her footing and began to slip. Xiaoxiao leapt up and grabbed her, but she was already in the water, the fishing-rod snapping in two as she fell. With great difficulty, Xiaoxiao managed to pull her back on to the rock. Her clothes were soaked through and both children were terrified. Xiaoxiao promptly asked her, 'Did you hurt yourself?' Sister looked at her wrist. 'I've scraped a piece of skin off this hand, but that doesn't matter. It's just that my clothes are all soaking wet. What are we going to do?' Seeing that she was close to tears, Xiaoxiao hastened to comfort her. 'Don't be afraid, I brought a towel. First you can wipe yourself, then we'll go and sit in the sun. You'll be dry in no time. If you go home and change your clothes, Aunt is sure to tell you off.' Sister thought for a moment, then followed him on to the bank.

Xiaoiao stood in the shade of a tree looking at Sister's face which had already been burned to a deep crimson. Sister said, 'I'm boiling. I feel really dizzy.' Xiaoxiao asked, 'Are your clothes dry yet?' Sister supported her head with her hands and retorted, 'How could they possibly dry out so fast?' Xiaoxiao said, 'I'll go home and fetch a parasol. That way you can shade your head while your clothes dry.' Sister nodded and Xiaoxiao quickly ran back home.

He couldn't find a parasol anywhere. Zhao Mama saw him and asked, 'Xiaoxiao, what are you looking for? Your Mama and Aunt are both having their afternoon nap, don't go rummaging through things and making such a racket.' Xiaoxiao had no option but to tell her quietly what had happened. Zhao Mama was alarmed. 'What sort of brilliant idea have you come up with! You'll end up giving your sister sunstroke!' She rushed out and carried Sister back to the house, found some dry clothes and put them on her. She felt Sister's burning forehead, then boiled some mung-bean soup for her to drink and made her sniff 'anti-sunstroke pills'. Then she took Sister in her arms and sat quietly with her under the verandah, not ceasing for a moment to scold Xiaoxiao for his thoughtlessness. Sister leant exhaustedly against Zhao Mama's shoulder and said, 'It wasn't Brother's fault. I fell in because of my own carelessness.' Xiaoxiao just stared blankly.

That evening Sister kept vomiting and could eat nothing. Aunt was beside herself with anxiety and Mother said that she was certainly suffering from sunstroke and they would call a doctor first thing next morning. Zhao Mama said nothing. Xiaoxiao was terrified, and it was not until the following morning when Sister appeared in perfect health that his burden of anxiety left him.

They didn't dare to go out again, so they just played in the courtyard. They pulled all the supportive bamboo stakes out of the morning glory and bound them into rectangular lattices, then arranged them together under the shade of a tree, leaving space for a door, to form a little bamboo hut. This kept the children busy all day, and it was not until the lamps were lit and Zhao Mama pressed them to come in for their evening meal that they stopped their work and went inside.

Mother smiled and said, 'Now that Sister is here, Xiaoxiao has a playmate and doesn't even bother about eating. What are you going to do tomorrow when Uncle comes to take Sister home?' Xiaoxiao just laughed and went on discussing with Sister how they were to finish building their cubby house.

The next day Xiaoxiao's school was to hold a 'scholastic achievements exhibition'. There was to be an assembly of staff and students in the morning and they were to sing the school song. Several of Xiaoxiao's schoofriends came to see him, wanting him to go with them, but Xiaoxiao was anxious to finish building the hut and unwilling to go at all. But his friends were insistent, so all he could do was give Sister a few brief instructions, then add, 'I'll be back after midday. You first fix the roof on.' Sister assented and he went off with his friends.

After what seemed an eternity, the masters arrived, the school song was sung and then disorder reigned for some time. Xiaoxiao didn't wait for the assembly to end, but slipped out on his own. Passing a bookshop, he bought a small silk national flag and elatedly carried it raised high all the way home. As soon as he got inside the door he called, 'Sister, I've bought a national flag to stick on the cubby house. . .' Zhao Mama came out from her room and said with a smile, 'Sister has gone.' Xiaoxiao glared at her. 'You can't trick me!' He leapt up on to the verandah and saw Mother sitting inside under the window writing a letter. He asked urgently, 'Where's Sister?' Mother put down her pen and said, 'Uncle came to fetch them this morning: They left on the 10 o'clock train.' Xiaoxiao stood stupefied: 'Why didn't you tell me before they were leaving?' Mother replied, 'Didn't I tell you yesterday evening? Uncle wrote a few days ago to say that he was taking five days' holiday and would come to take the family to a new home in the south – I didn't think they would go so soon either. Sister didn't want to leave at first, but Auntie said they were pressed for time and still had to go back and pack things for the move. I couldn't pressure them to stay.' Xiaoxiao said, 'Why didn't Zhao Mama go to school and call me home?' 'Everyone was too busy. Who still had time to think of that?' Mother said, then resumed her letter-writing. Xiaoxiao stood for a long time in silence, then went out and sat vacantly under the verandah, the flag still grasped in one hand.

That afternoon Xiaoxiao took a long nap and didn't get up until dusk. He ate a hasty meal, then sat dejectedly under the lamplight. Zhao Mama came in and asked, 'Where are my scissors?' Xiaoxiao said, 'I haven't seen them.' Zhao Mama asked, 'Didn't you and Sister take them yesterday to cut string for binding bamboo lattices?' Xiaoxiao remembered, 'They're hanging on a branch of the tree in the corner of the courtyard. You go and get them yourself.' As Zhao Mama went out, Mother said, 'I've never known a child as naughty as you. You make free with anything that comes to hand. I thought it was strange that the morning glory all collapsed yesterday, I never imagined that you had pulled all the stakes out. If this goes on, you'll be demolishing the house next! Now that Sister's gone, you should revise your lessons. Just playing all day is simply not good enough!' Xiaoxiao's melancholy heart had no place to vent its feelings, but hearing Mother's reproaches, he took the opportunity to sink down on the table and weep. Mother ignored him.

After crying for a while he became bored and stood up to go to bed. Mother went with him, made up his bed and gently stroked his hair saying, 'Have a good sleep. Get up early tomorrow morning and I'll help you to write a letter to Sister inviting her to come next year.' He fought back his sobs and assented, then lay down. Mother sat at his bedside until she thought he was asleep, then turned out the lamp and went out.

He sat up again – how bright the moonlight was outside his window! It illuminated the courtyard, the morning glory that now sprawled all over the ground, and the unfinished bamboo hut standing at the corner of the wall. The little door was half open and the woven roof was already in place – that was Sister's work. . .

He listlessly got up and closed the curtain, then lay down again – the faint murmuring of the stream behind the house and the rustling of the wind in the trees brought the memories flooding back. He pillowed his head in his hands and looked at his pyjamas and bedclothes shining snowy-white in the moonlight. A light breeze wafted through the window and he couldn't help once more burying his face in his pillow and sobbing.

―――――

Now the moon had gone, the water had gone, Sister had gone and the bamboo hut had gone. They had all ceased to exist. All that remained was the lonely grief of the universe that engulfed his childish soul.

24 July 1922
Translated by R. A. Roberts

EARLY SUMMER

YU RU

SPRING HAD ALREADY passed. The loveliest and most enchanting season in south China had arrived with astonishing speed. The cool southern breeze, the brilliant clouds that glowed rosy pink at dawn and sunset, the thick, lush greenery that covered mountains and valleys, and the incessant chirrup of insects through the night, all made one realize it was already early summer.

That afternoon, my young son returned from kindergarten with a note requesting that families send unwanted odds and ends of cloth for making toys for the Children's Day Festival on 1 June. The teachers and assistants there thought of everything – since the kindergarten had been established, we mothers had paid little attention to presents for Children's Day.

From outside the window, the sound of sprinkling water reached my ears, and I knew that my son was busy at the first of his afternoon household tasks – watering the roses and jasmine. I should take a break too.

I left my work and went outside. In the rosy light of the setting sun, the child was busy at work among the rose-bushes. His little face, covered with perspiration, was even more pink, fresh and tender than the roses.

I sat down under the front verandah enjoying the cool summer evening breeze. An intoxicating fragrance filled my senses. This was not the scent of rose or jasmine. I raised my head and gazed upwards – ah! – the tree was flowering. She is summer's messenger, announcing to all that summer is on its way.

I leaned on the verandah post looking up at the bailan tree. It was tall, straight and sturdy. Here and there amongst the emerald-green leaves, flowers like white jade had burst into blossom. Ah! And hidden beneath the leaves I could see myriads of tiny, tender buds. This year it would blossom more luxuriantly than ever. Throughout the long southern summer, it would send its delicate fragrance wafting through my window.

I looked at the child catching crickets among the rose-bushes and my thoughts flew back to the time when the tree was planted. He wasn't even born then, and my young daughter had just begun to wear the brilliant red neckerchief of the youth corps. On Children's Day, she and I had planted the bailan tree together. In the twinkling of an eye, six years had passed. That year the tree had not even reached my daughter's shoulder, but now it was level with the eaves of the roof.

I glanced at my watch. It was almost six o'clock and my daughter had still not come home from school. A wave of anxiety made me realize that the real reason why I had put down my work and come outside to rest, look at the flowers and enjoy the wind, was because I was waiting for her. Recently we had spent very little time together – she seemed to be even more busy than me. Every evening she would hastily finish her meal, then go out again, and I had no idea what it was she was doing. . .

I gazed along the village path into the distance, and far away could make out a slender figure approaching. Here she was. She walked very slowly as if deep in thought, her school bag carelessly slung on her back and her long plaits swaying gently. I suddenly felt: she's growing very fast this year, just like the early blossoms on the bailan tree, she has already entered the most beautiful season of life.

My son gave a delighted cry of greeting and bounded away like a young deer to meet his sister. She squatted down and opened her arms to embrace him, a little bunch of purple wild flowers quivering in her hand. I heard an indistinct stream of words and laughter, then hand in hand they appeared before me. My daughter smiled and greeted me: 'Mama!'

'Why are you so late?' I asked.

The smile faded from her face. Offering only, 'I had things to do at school,' she pushed away her brother's hand and went into the house.

When we went back indoors, I saw she was filling a glass with water for her flowers. I said, 'Those flowers only last for one day. They'll wither so quickly it's not worth putting them in water.'

She glanced at me disapprovingly. 'Then we should appreciate them while we can, we shouldn't overlook their one day of beauty!' She placed the glass of flowers on the dining-table, instructing her brother, 'You're not to touch them!'

I remembered that in the past she had always liked to chop wild flowers into tiny pieces when playing 'houses' with her friends. When had she begun to treasure flowers like this?

While we were eating, she suddenly exclaimed, 'Drat! I've left Chen Xiaoping's letter at school. I'll have to go and get it straight away.'

Chen Xiaoping had been her best friend at lower-middle school, but when they were promoted to upper-middle school she had transferred elsewhere. However, the two girls still maintained a close friendship, and frequently wrote to each other.

'What are you so worried about?' I asked. 'The two of you write to each other every couple of days. What does it matter if you lose one letter? You can't possibly keep them all anyway.'

'Really Mama! She wrote me a secret. I'm the only one that knows!'

I couldn't help laughing. Ever since they were small, the children had loved to have secrets: where they had buried a coloured bead; who had been given a beautiful silk ribbon . . . they were all secrets; sometimes I had been given instructions from many different children to keep the same secret. . .

But seeing my amusement, my daughter became angry. 'Hey, hey, what do you think you're doing picking up food with your hands?' she crossly admonished her little brother.

My son had only just begun to learn to use chopsticks and was still far from expert, but he was determined to display his abilities and tried to pick up a piece of steaming egg. He managed with some difficulty to pick up a tiny piece, but before he could get it to his dish, it fell on to his sister's sleeve. She chided him angrily, 'Just use a spoon and have done with it!'

'Teacher said I'm big now and can't use a spoon to eat with. That's what little kids use.'

'And how old are you?' she scoffed at him.

'I'm already five!' he replied with righteous self-assurance.

I remembered the note from the kindergarten. 'Oh, that's right! Last year I forgot to give you presents on Children's Day. What would you like this year? You can choose yourselves.'

'I want a toy tractor!' my son cried jubilantly, then asked, 'Sister, what do you want?'

'I don't want anything. Do you think I'm still a kid?' she replied in all seriousness.

Her expression made me laugh again. I still remember clearly how each year she had anxiously longed for her present. And the look of exultant joy on her face when she received it was still fresh in my memory. Once, by coincidence, everyone had given her wooden animals. That evening she had laid out building blocks under the lamplight to make a zoo, and enclosed each of the little deer and horses in its own cage. She enjoyed herself so much that she refused to go to sleep. Another time I took her to a children's bookstore to buy her some picture story-books. She read through dozens of them on the spot, yet chose for herself a volume of Pushkin's children's verses. . .

I was going to ask her what she would really like this year, but she had already put down her bowl and gone into her own room.

Seeing that his sister had gone, my son, now at ease, boldly took up his spoon and rapidly finished off the whole plate of steamed eggs.

My daughter came out of her room. She had changed her clothes, tidied her hair and tied silk ribbons on her plaits. 'Mama, I'm going now' she said coolly.

'But you've barely finished your meal. What are you rushing off for?'

'I've got things to do at school.'

I sighed. 'I've got things to do at school' again! It seemed that no matter how many times I asked her, that was all I would ever get in reply.

———

After my son had finished eating, he went off by himself to wash his hands, and then began to pester me: 'Mama, aren't you going to go for a walk?'

I felt somewhat perplexed. Just what was it that was keeping my daughter so busy recently? In the past she'd pestered me to go for a stroll too, but now she scarcely even spoke to me. I ought to go and speak to her class teacher and find out what was going on.

Once outside, the little fellow made a new request: 'Mama, let's climb the mountain.'

'No, no, it's almost dark.'

'Don't be scared, I'll look after you!' he said valiantly, picking up a twig that was lying on the ground.

I laughed and took him by the hand. One by one we climbed the stone steps that led up the mountain behind the house. The tips of the pine trees were dyed a brilliant gold by the setting sun, and flocks of calling birds were flying home to roost; the sky had already turned a dim violet.

After walking for some time, we heard the sound of singing.

'Who could that be singing?'

'It's Sister!' my son said with certainty.

'Rubbish! Hasn't she gone back to school?'

'Uhh . . . well, it's her singing anyway.'

He was right. As we got closer, I could clearly recognize my daughter's voice. Usually she very rarely sang, and always sang particularly badly in front of other people, because she was shy. But today her voice was gentle and lively, indicating that she was in the best of spirits. I looked towards the back of the mountain in the direction from which the singing was coming, and in a clearing in the forest saw two girls busy watering a newly established patch of peanut plants. Now they sprinkled water, and now they bent down to catch insects, singing all the time. The turquoise ribbons my daughter had tied on to the end of her plaits danced among the peanut leaves like a pair of butterflies.

So she'd been coming up here to work! But why get all dressed up? I wondered. I pulled my son to a halt, not wanting to let him disturb the two girls who were immersed in the joys of physical labour. But suddenly he heard a cricket chirruping from a crack in the rocks, and quickly turning back, began to tiptoe towards the grass-covered rocks from which the sound was coming. . .

19

I stood motionless under a pine tree, wanting to listen to my daughter's voice, but they had already stopped singing. I heard her say with a happy laugh, 'Oh Lili, what a lovely evening! How could we have lived here for so many years without discovering what a beautiful place this is? Look at the evening clouds, the distant mountains, the Pearl River . . . what wonderful scenery!'

Following her voice, I gazed at the evening clouds, the flowing water, the distant mountains . . . yes, the scenery was beautiful, but hadn't I often brought her up on to the mountain before? I used to admire the view while she picked flowers, caught butterflies and collected pine nuts just like the little boy who was now wriggling through the tall grass. The scenery had never held any fascination for her. It looked as though the child had grown up.

A burst of merry laughter flew past me from the small path above my head. The two girls, hand in hand, were climbing up to a little pavilion. I was concealed from them by the thick curtain of pine needles overhead.

'When I came out Mama asked where I was going and I said I had something to do at school!' a voice said with a laugh.

'Shouldn't you have told her?' the second voice asked anxiously.

'What? Of course not! This patch of peanuts is our contribution for when we join the Youth League. How can we tell people about it now?'

'You're right, whatever happens we mustn't let the secret get out!'

Standing under the pine tree, I couldn't help smiling to myself. So their secrets now had an entirely new content. No wonder she was so busy!

'Hey! Let's sing a song.'

'OK, which one?'

'What do you want to sing?'

'Let's both think of a song, and on the count of three start singing together. See if we pick the same song.'

'OK. . .' A short silence followed.

I anxiously turned to locate my son, but he had already moved even further off. I quietly walked several paces forward and sat down on a rock. From here I could see the pavilion. My daughter and her schoolfriend were standing in front of the pavilion, their arms around the pillars, gazing at the river and the evening clouds. Their eyes sparkled mischievously. . .

'OK, one, two, three. . . .'

Their voices, like two sets of silver bells, began to sing simultaneously:

'Sun . . . yoh . . . ah!'

They were singing a song from the opera *Red Clouds*. In order to protect the Red Army, Red Clouds had led the enemy along a side road away from the communist troops. But her ruse had been discovered, and she had sung this song after being shot and wounded; the girls' voices expressed her hatred for the enemy, her love for the Red Army, her longing for life and her grief at the early loss of her youth. . . . They sang slowly with the joy of victory and the sorrow of the young girl. Their singing moved me deeply: no, this was not the singing of children, no child could give such profound expression to the complex emotions embodied in this song.

The sky had become even darker and the wind whistling through the pines sounded like the roaring of waves. Soft whispers drifted down to me from the little pavilion. . .

'Do you know? Chen Xiaoping wrote to say that she and one of the boys in her class. . .'

A burst of giggles filled the summer night. When it subsided, the second voice pursued the question.

'And what about you then?'

'I don't have any secrets,' my daughter emphasized each word.

'You haven't? Then who put a letter in your drawer at noon today?'

'That wasn't a letter, it was a note!'

'That makes no difference, it was something that couldn't be said in front of other people anyway.'

'Why shouldn't it be said in front of other people? He was only telling me to meet him in the reading room at eight o'clock tonight to discuss editing our 4 May wall-newspaper.'

'Then why did he write a note? Why didn't he tell you directly? Huh? Huh?'

My daughter was silent for a moment. I guessed she was smiling.

'It is strange! He's afraid to talk to me, and if he does say a word or two he doesn't know where to look. He doesn't even dare to glance at me. . .'

'Afraid to talk to you and look at you? Then why has he arranged to meet you to talk about the wall-newspaper?'

'Oh, you're rotten, I won't tell you my secrets again!'

'Haha, so it is a secret?'

Their laughter mingled in the air and the two girls were probably giggling in each other's arms. Unfortunately the sky was already dark and I could no longer distinguish their movements.

My son approached through the darkness, a cricket chirruping in his hands. He called out excitedly, 'Mama, let's go!'

We leisurely retraced our steps down the mountain. The moon had risen and when I turned to look back, I saw the pines and the little pavilion amongst the trees veiled in moonlight. Indistinctly, I could make out two figures seated on the pavilion steps. I was certain they were looking at the moon and feeling that this moon, this moonlit night was the most beautiful and enchanting they had ever seen.

Back at home, I put my son to bed and then sat down to do some work. But I could not settle down, so I went back outside to sit alone under the bailan tree by the verandah. . . .

The moon rose higher and the night was filled with the chirruping of insects as if my daughter was there whispering quietly to her schoolfriend. But I knew she had already gone back to school and was discussing the wall-newspaper with the boy who didn't dare to look at her. Yes: their secrets were already so much more complex than before that even Mama had to be deceived now. But why couldn't Mama understand that this child had already grown up, had already entered a new stage of life? Why was it that suddenly we had no common language?

The cool wind rustled through the thick foliage of the bailan tree, wafting its sweet fragrance into my face. Since it had been planted, five Children's Days had passed. How many children in red neckerchiefs who had planted trees then were now growing up like this young tree and already considering what their contributory gift should be on entering the Youth League? These children, fostered in China's new society, were just like the bailan tree – upright, pure, free and unconstrained. Interfused with the years of their youth were lofty ideals and beautiful illusions. Thus they took life more seriously than adults and were more sensitive to its lovely radiance. . .

Ah – how could I understand them? Our youth had been so different. Suddenly events of twenty-five years ago sprung unwittingly to my mind. . .

It was also a summer night – in my home town. A crowd of barefoot girls, hoes on their shoulders and carrying bamboo baskets, had just come down from the mountain. We had climbed the hills at dusk to dig bamboo shoots, pick bean pods and gather wild flowers. Now the group had dispersed leaving only myself and Suying, the child-bride of a rich peasant family, sitting together on the bank of a stream swollen with the spring rains. I took a wild flower I had picked on the hillside and slipped it into her hair above one of her long plaits. I laughed delightedly: 'Oh, you look lovely – just like a new bride!'

She snatched the flower from her hair and threw it into the stream. It floated away on the churning water. I gazed at my fifteen-year-old companion and saw that her childish face was streaked with tears. She asked me angrily, 'You think I'm really going to be a new bride?'

I had unwittingly stirred her most painful feelings. In another three days, she was to be formally married. Her husband was only two years her senior, yet he already beat her in the roughest way.

'Then what are you going to do? Get your mother to buy you back?'

'My mother is too poor to even feed herself. Yesterday she told the messenger boy that she had hired herself out as a casual labourer and can't come to my wedding, but I know perfectly well that she has no money to buy a wedding present and is too embarrassed to come! In any case I've decided that I'm not going to marry him.'

It was true, Suying's in-laws were comparatively well-off. I'd heard that they were planning a splendid banquet for their son's wedding. I fell silent, not knowing how to comfort this friend with whom I had played since childhood. The stream sparkled in the moonlight, the chirping of insects filled the air. The night was peaceful and the breeze cool, yet a nameless terror seemed to oppress our heavy hearts.

Suddenly I heard a splash from the pool behind us. I leapt up in fright and looked timidly in the direction of the sound, but all I could see was the glow of fireflies flitting across the water. . .

Suying heaved a sigh and said in a low voice, 'The water spirit is looking for a substitute body.'

I felt the terror beginning to rise in me, and hastily grabbed up our baskets: 'Let's go home! Huh? How come you've only dug out these few bamboo shoots? You're sure to be scolded by your mother-in-law when you get back. Here, take all of mine.'

'Let her curse!' Suying said stubbornly, then after a moment added, 'What are you afraid of? The water spirit is only a person changed into a ghost – no, driven to become a ghost!'

Who would have guessed that the following evening the whole village would be in uproar? They said that Suying had taken the dishes and chopsticks for her wedding feast to wash them in the stream, where she had somehow lost her footing and drowned. . .

That evening I lay sleepless with terror. Through the still night I could hear a woman wailing – it was Suying's mother calling back the spirit of her dead daughter. They used to say that if a wronged soul was not called back by a relative it would never be able to return home. . .

I peeped out of the window of my upper room. Holding in her hand a dimly glowing paper lantern, the woman was moving along the bank of the stream, crying Suying's name and calling to her to come home. The light disappeared into the distance and all I could hear was the rise and fall of her desolate cries. Suddenly another splash sounded from the pool. I hastily closed the wooden lattice windows and buried myself under the bedclothes, Suying's furious voice echoing in my ears: 'The water spirit is only a person changed into a ghost – no, driven to become a ghost!' Was Suying also looking for a substitute body, then?

I shivered, and the unhappy past vanished like a dream. The night was as cool as water and the moonlight like frost. The scent of the bailan tree on this summer night was so sweet and strong that it seemed as if all the strength it had accumulated during the cold winter months was bursting forth in this wonderful aroma.

People used to say that everything must come to an end sometime, and only hatred is eternal. Now the old society, which specialized in creating suffering, had ended. I believed that Suying's fury, too, had already abated. For today's youth live in a bright, pure, spiritual world unshadowed by demons and monsters.

I was just about to get up and go indoors when on the moonlit path I saw two figures approaching. They stopped where the path began to curve towards our house, and I heard a boy's voice say, 'I'll go back now. Don't forget – tomorrow evening at 7.00.'

'I won't forget. Thanks.' That was my daughter's voice. She stood on the path and raised a little bunch of something she held in her hand in farewell. 'See you tomorrow!'

A few minutes later she appeared skipping and hopping before me, humming a little tune. As she caught sight of me, she stopped in happy astonishment and involuntarily caught her breath. 'Mama, you're still up!'

Now I could see clearly that she was carrying a sprig of bailan blossom in her hand. 'Um, Who brought you home?'

'A . . . schoolfriend,' she replied with a laugh, throwing me a rapid glance.

'Why are you so late?'

'I had things to do at school,' she answered as usual. Then after a moment's thought added, 'I'll be late tomorrow too, don't wait up for me.'

'What? You haven't finished discussing the 4 May wall-newspaper?' I asked without thinking.

She cried out in astonishment, 'Oh, Mama, how did you know?' Then she suddenly giggled and leaping forward threw her arms around my neck. 'I can't keep any secrets from you! You're a wicked Mama!'

I laughed and pushed her inside the house. In a moment she had become a child again. I was longing to say that I knew many more secrets than that – more than she could possibly imagine. I also wanted to tell her about those events of the past that had suddenly come to mind, but in the end I said nothing. Seeing her laughing so happily under the lamplight, I didn't have the heart to disturb her pure, bright heart with the sufferings of wronged spirits in the old society.

She was just about to put her spray of flowers into a vase when I said, 'Will you give them to me? Let me have them on my desk.'

'I'll put them there for you,' she assented with a smile, and went with me into the study. 'Oh, greedy Mama, it's fragrant enough in here as it is! Look, you've got the whole bailan tree outside your window.'

She turned on the desk lamp and put the flowers into a vase for me. Then, humming a tune, she turned to leave. Suddenly she turned back with a mischievous smile: 'Actually, it doesn't matter if I do tell you. Mama, you've got it wrong. Tomorrow we're not going to discuss the wall-newspaper, tomorrow I'm going to Youth League classes. The . . . classmate who was with me just now is our League branch secretary.'

'You're right. I had got things wrong,' I said. 'In fact Children's Day is not your festival any more, 4 May is your festival. Come, dear, let me congratulate you – you have already left childhood and entered youth.'

'Really Mama! . . . In fact for us, which day isn't a festival?' She laughed a little shyly and hurriedly slipped out, closing the door behind her. But she left in my room a peal of merry laughter.

29 May 1962
Translated by R. A. Roberts

L I L I E S

RU ZHIJUAN

Mid-autumn 1946.

THE DECISION WAS made that day that the troops fighting in the coastal region would launch a general offensive that evening. The other comrades from the production office of our arts ensemble were all assigned work in various combat companies by the commander of the main offensive regiment, but, probably because I was a woman, the commander scratched his head in perplexity for a long time before finally calling a courier to lead me to a first-aid post near the front lines.

I didn't mind being assigned to a first-aid post. Just as long as I wasn't being ushered into a strongbox, I was willing to do anything. I shouldered my pack and set off after the courier.

That morning there had been a shower of rain, and although the sky was now clear, the road was still extremely slippery. But the crops on either side of the track had been washed a brilliant emerald-green and sparkled like jewels in the sunlight. The air carried a fresh, moist fragrance. If it hadn't been for the intermittent explosions of the enemy's blind cannon-fire, I might have imagined myself on the way to market.

The courier walked ahead of me with rapid strides, and right from the start I lagged behind him some fifty or sixty metres. My feet were festering and the road so slippery that no matter how hard I tried, I couldn't catch up with him. I thought of calling to him to wait for me, but I was afraid he would laugh at me for being a frightened coward, and didn't dare. I really was afraid that I wouldn't be able to find the first-aid post on my own. I began to feel angry with him.

But strange to say, he seemed to have eyes in the back of his head, and stopped at the roadside of his own accord, though he kept his face to the front and didn't even glance at me. When I had almost struggled up to where he stood, he set off again by himself, and in a short time had once more left me far behind. I genuinely didn't have the strength to keep up, so simply staggered on slowly behind him. However, it was not so bad this time; he didn't let me lag too far back but he never let me get close to him either, always maintaining the distance between us. If I walked quickly, he would stride on ahead, and if I walked slowly, he would vacillate to the right and left before me. What was strange was that I never saw him look back once. I couldn't help feeling rather intrigued by this courier.

I hadn't paid him any attention at the regiment headquarters just now, but by the look of his tall, slender figure and broad shoulders he was a strong young fellow. He wore a faded yellow uniform and puttees that reached to his knees. Several leafy twigs stuck into the barrel of the rifle on his shoulder seemed more a decoration than a means of camouflage.

I hadn't caught up with him, but my swollen feet were burning like twin fires. I suggested to him that we rest for a while, and sat down on a stone at the edge of a field. He sat down with his back to me on another stone a good distance away, acting as if I simply didn't exist. From experience I knew that this was because I was a woman. Women comrades who worked at company level always had these problems. Slightly irritated, I displayed my spirit of resistance by walking over and sitting down directly opposite him. Now I could see his round, childish face. He must have been eighteen at the most. Seeing me sit down near him, he immediately became as alarmed as if a time bomb had been planted nearby. He was clearly ill at ease, knowing that to turn his head away would be impolite, but too embarrassed to face in my direction. He thought of standing up, but then felt that that would make things even more awkward. Fighting hard not to laugh, I casually asked him where he was from. He didn't answer immediately. He blushed a deep crimson like the painted face of the god of war, and only after stuttering incoherently for a while did he manage to make it clear that he was from the Tianmu Mountains. So we were from the same area!

'What do you do at home?'

'I haul bamboo.'

Looking at his broad shoulders, a vision of a green, misty sea of bamboo floated before my eyes. Through the trees a narrow, stone-stepped mountain path wound upwards out of sight. A broad-shouldered young man with an old piece of blue cloth cushioning his shoulder was hauling several thick bamboos down the mountain. The tips of the bamboos trailed on the ground far behind him, issuing a rhythmic thud as they fell from step to step. This was the hometown life with which I was so familiar! My heart immediately warmed towards him. I questioned him further.

'How old are you?'

'Nineteen.'

'When did you join the revolution?'

'A year ago.'

'How did you come to join the revolution?' At this point I suddenly felt that this was more like an interrogation than a conversation, but I still couldn't resist questioning him.

'When the Communist troops pulled out of Jiangnan,* I followed them.'

'How many in your family?'

'Mum, Dad, younger brothers and sisters, and another girl who lives with us.'

'You're not married yet?'

He blushed scarlet and became even more disconcerted, his fingers endlessly counting the eyelets on his belt. After a long pause, he lowered his head with a bashful grin, and shook his head.

* After the surrender of the Japanese in 1945, the Chinese Communist Party held peace talks with the Nationalist Party in an effort to bring peace to the nation. The Communists also withdrew troops from Jiangnan (southern Jiangsu and Anhui Provinces and northern Zhejiang Province). But shortly afterwards the Nationalists reneged on the agreement and launched large-scale attacks on the Communist-liberated areas.

I was going to ask him if he had a fiancée, but seeing the flustered state he was in, swallowed my words.

We sat in silence for a while, then he raised his head and looked at the sky, glancing at me to indicate that we should be on our way.

When I stood up to go, I saw him take off his cap and covertly mop the sweat with a towel. This was all my fault – he hadn't shed a drop of perspiration marching along the road, but his conversation with me had brought the sweat pouring off him.

When we arrived at the first-aid station, it was already past two in the afternoon. The first-aid post had been set up in a primary school about a mile from the battle front. Six buildings of various sizes were arranged in a rough triangle with a yard in the centre overgrown with weeds. Obviously the school had been closed for some time. When we arrived, several health workers were preparing gauze bandages and cotton wool. The rooms were filled with doors propped up on piles of bricks that were to serve as hospital beds.

We hadn't been there long when a county cadre arrived. His eyes were heavily bloodshot from lack of sleep, and he had stuck a piece of card under the front of his tattered felt cap to shade them from the sunlight. He came in puffing and panting, with a rifle on one shoulder and a steelyard on the other, a basket of eggs in his left hand and a large cooking pot in his right. Putting down the things he had brought, he apologized to us and at the same time poured out his troubles. Gulping breathlessly from drinking down a cup of water, he pulled a lump of cooked rice from inside his jacket and took a large bite. I was so astonished by the speed with which he did all this that I didn't catch what he was saying. He seemed to be saying that we would have to go and borrow cotton quilts ourselves. One of the health workers told me that the army quilts had still not been issued, but because it was essential that the wounded be kept warm, we would have to borrow quilts from the villagers. Even if we could only get a dozen or so strips of quilt padding, that would be better than nothing. I had been feeling frustrated at not being able to lend a hand, so I volunteered to undertake the task, and, afraid that I wouldn't have time to complete it on my own, randomly asked my townsman to help me mobilize a few households before he went back. After a moment's hesitation, he followed me out of the door.

We went first to a nearby village, he covering the eastern side and I the western. In a short time I had written out three receipts and borrowed two strips of cotton padding and one cotton quilt. My arms were full and I was elated. I was just going to take the bedding back to the first-aid post and come back for more, when the courier, his arms empty, came up from the opposite direction.

'What? You couldn't borrow any?' I was puzzled. I felt that the villagers' political awareness here was very high. They were also very open-hearted. How could he possibly have not borrowed any?

'Comrade, you go and borrow them . . . the villagers here are strictly feudal. . .'

'Which house? You take me there.' I guessed that he had certainly said something inappropriate and put the people's backs up. Not being able to borrow a cotton quilt was a trifling matter, but to offend the ordinary people was of serious concern. I called him to take me to have a look, but he stubbornly lowered his head and stood as if nailed to the spot, unwilling to move. I went over to him and in a low voice explained to him the importance of making a good impression on the masses. Hearing what I said, without further ado, he led me to the house.

When we entered the courtyard, we found the main room of the house empty. The door to the inner room, which was screened by a piece of blue cloth on a red yoke, was framed to the right and left with an antithetical couplet written on bright red paper. We had no choice but to stand outside calling out 'Elder Sister', 'Sister-in-law'. There was no answer, but there was the sound of movement within. After a moment the curtain was flicked aside, and a young woman appeared. She was very attractive: her eyebrows curved gracefully above a high-bridged nose, and a soft fringe covered her forehead. Although her clothes were of coarse cloth, they were all new.

Seeing that her hair was done up in the stiff bun of a married woman, I addressed her as 'Elder Sister-in-law', and apologized to her, asking her not to take offence if this comrade had said something out of turn when he was here just now. She stood there listening with her face turned away slightly and a smile on her tightly closed lips. She didn't make a sound, even when I stopped speaking, but kept her head down, biting her lips as if holding back gales of laughter about something incredibly amusing. Now I began to feel awkward. What should I say next? I glanced at the courier at my side, and saw him gazing at me unblinkingly as if watching the company commander giving a demonstration. All I could do was brace myself and somewhat sheepishly ask if we could borrow the quilt, explaining that the troops of the Communist Party were fighting for the ordinary people. As I talked she stopped smiling and listened carefully, glancing towards the house now and then. When I fell silent, she looked first at me and then at the courier as if weighing up my words, then after long consideration, turned and went into the house to fetch the quilt.

The courier seized this opportunity to express his indignation. 'That's exactly what I said just now, but she wouldn't lend it to me. Don't you think it's strange?'

I hastily threw him a disdainful glance to stop him talking, but it was already too late. The young woman with the quilt had already reached the doorway. As soon as I saw the quilt I understood why she had been so reluctant to lend it just now: it was completely new. The cover was of wine-coloured synthetic satin, patterned all over with white lilies. As if deliberately wanting to annoy the courier, she held the quilt out to me saying, 'Here, take it!'

My arms were already full of quilts, so I motioned to the courier with my lips that he should take it. Quite unexpectedly, he gazed up at the sky, pretending that he hadn't seen, and I was obliged to call to him before he finally took it with eyes cast down and a look of displeasure on his face. Highly flustered, he turned on his heel and shot out of the street door. But as he passed the door, we heard a sharp ripping sound as his uniform caught on the door hook, leaving a sizeable piece of torn cloth hanging down from his shoulder. The young woman burst out laughing and hastily searched out a needle and cotton to stitch it up for him, but he wouldn't allow it on any account, and left with the quilt under his arm.

We hadn't gone far when someone told us that the young woman was a new bride of only three days. This quilt was her entire dowry. I began to feel sorry that we had borrowed it, and the courier knitted his brows too, gazing silently at the quilt in his arms. I guessed he felt the same way as I did. Sure enough, as we walked along he began to mutter, 'We didn't understand the situation. It's really not right to borrow someone's bridal quilt!' I couldn't resist playing a joke on him, and deliberately assumed a serious air. 'You're right! Who knows how many mornings she got up early and how many evenings she stayed up late doing extra jobs to save up for this quilt? For all we know she might have spent sleepless night on account of it. But some people still curse her as strictly feudal. . .'

Hearing this, he suddenly halted, and after a moment's silence said, 'Then . . . then let's take it back to her!'

'Since we've already borrowed it, to take it back now would only hurt her feelings.' His earnest, embarrassed expression was both amusing and endearing. Unaccountably, I had already given my heart to this simple young townsfellow of mine.

Hearing that my explanation seemed reasonable, he thought for a moment, then said resolutely, 'OK, then we'll leave it at that, but when we've finished with it we must wash it really clean for her.' Having made this decision, he grabbed all the quilts out of my arms and with them hung over his shoulders went striding off at a rapid pace.

Back at the first-aid post, I told him to return to the regimental headquarters. He brightened up immediately, and after giving me a farewell salute, raced off. He had only gone a few paces when he suddenly thought of something, and feeling around in his shoulder bag pulled out two steamed bread rolls which he waved at me, then placed on a boulder at the roadside. 'Have something to eat!' he called, then sped off, his feet scarcely touching the ground. I went over to pick up the two hard, dry rolls, and noticed that at some time a wild chrysanthemum had been added to the greenery in his rifle barrel, and was now nodding at his ear.

He was already disappearing into the distance, but I could still see that torn patch of cloth hanging from his shoulder flapping in the breeze. I regretted not stitching it up for him before he had left. Now he would have to spend at least one night with a bared shoulder.

There were very few staff to run the first-aid post, so the county cadre mobilized several of the village women to fetch water, boil the cauldrons and do various other odd jobs. Our young woman came as well, smiling with closed lips as she had before. She occasionally stole a glance at me from the corner of her eye, but she frequently looked around her as if searching for something. Finally she asked me outright, 'Where has that little comrade gone?' I told her he wasn't a member of the staff here and had gone to the front lines. She laughed in embarrassment and said, 'When he came to borrow the quilt just now, I'm afraid he felt the sharp edge of my tongue!' She closed her lips in another smile, then set to work to lay the borrowed quilts and cotton padding out neatly on the doors and tables (two tables side by side served as a bed). I saw her put her own new lily-patterned quilt on a door outside under the eaves.

Night fell and a full moon rose above the horizon. Our general offensive had not yet been launched. As usual the enemy, dreading the night, had set great patches of the countryside ablaze and was continuing its barrage of blind shelling. Flare after flare was fired into the sky, nakedly exposing everything on the ground as if countless kerosene lamps had been lit under the moon. To launch an attack on a bright night like this presented enormous difficulties and would have to be paid for at considerable cost. I even began to hate that clear, bright moon.

The county cadre returned, bringing us several home-made dried-vegetable moon-cakes as a reward for our labours. It had slipped my mind that today was Mid-autumn Festival.

Ah – Mid-autumn Festival! At this moment outside every door in my home village would be placed a table on which was arranged incense, candles and several dishes of candied melon moon-cakes. The children would be impatiently longing for the incense to burn out so as to divide the things laid out for the enjoyment of the Moon Girl as soon as possible. They would be hopping and skipping beside the table and singing, 'Moon, moon, bright and dandy, beat the gongs and buy some candy' . . . or perhaps, 'Moon, moon is our nanny, shines on you and shines on me. . .' Thinking of the children, my thoughts turned to my young fellow townsman; several years ago the young man who hauled bamboos might very well have sung just those songs!. . . I took a bite of the delicious home-made moon-cake and thought that he was probably at this moment lying behind the fortifications or at the regimental command post – or maybe he was running through those winding communication trenches.

A short time later our cannons sounded and several red signal flares streaked through the sky. The attack had begun. Not long afterwards an intermittent stream of wounded men began to arrive at the first-aid post, and the atmosphere immediately became tense.

I took a notebook and began to register their names and units. Those with light wounds I could ask, but for the severely wounded I had to find their identification tags or look for a name on the inside of their jackets. Pulling out the identification tag of one badly wounded soldier, the word 'courier' sent a sudden shiver down my spine, and my heart began to pound. Only after I had pulled myself together did I see below it, 'X Battalion'. Ah! It wasn't him. My townsfellow was the regimental headquarters courier. But I felt an unaccountable desire to ask someone: might there be any wounded on the battlefield who had been missed? Apart from carrying messages, what else did couriers do on the battlefield? I didn't know myself why I should be asking these meaningless questions.

For the first hour or so of battle everything went smoothly. The wounded brought with them news that we had crossed the abatis; we had crossed the wire entanglement; we had occupied the enemy's front line fortifications and driven the assault into the town. But then the news suddenly stopped. The wounded coming in would only answer briefly, 'We're still fighting', or, 'We're fighting in the streets'. But from their mud-covered bodies, their look of utter exhaustion and even from the stretchers that looked as if they had been just dug out of a mud pit, everyone was well aware just what kind of battle was being fought at the front.

The first-aid post ran out of stretchers, and several badly wounded men who should have been sent immediately to the rear area hospital were unavoidably delayed. We could do nothing to relieve their pain, all we could do was wash their hands and faces with the aid of the village women, feed the ones who could eat, and put dry clothes on those who still carried their knapsacks. For some of them we also had to undo their clothing and wipe their bodies clean of mud and clotting blood.

I was accustomed to this kind of work, but the village women were both bashful and frightened. They were unwilling to touch the wounded men, and vied for the task of boiling the cauldrons – particularly that young bride. I talked to her for a long time before she assented with a blush, but she would only agree to be my assistant.

The sound of gunfire from the front had already become sporadic, and it felt as if dawn should soon break, yet it was only midnight. Outside the moon shone brilliantly, and seemed to have risen higher in the sky than usual. Another badly wounded soldier was brought in from the front. The beds inside were all filled, so I directed that he be put on the door outside under the eaves. The stretcher bearers lifted him on to the makeshift bed, but remained at his side, unwilling to leave. An elderly stretcher-bearer seized me by the shoulder, thinking I was a doctor. 'Doctor! Whatever happens you must find a way to save this comrade. If you can save him, I . . . our whole stretcher bearer corps will publicly commend you. . .' As he spoke, I discovered that all the other stretcher bearers were also gazing at me unblinkingly, as if a nod of my head would bring the wounded man instantaneous recovery. I wanted to explain the situation to them, but the young bride who had just approached the bed-head with a bowl of water, suddenly gave a short scream. I pushed them aside and found myself looking down at a round, childish face, its once ruddy brown skin now an ashen yellow. His eyes were serenely closed, and at his shoulder, below the gaping hole in his uniform, that piece of torn cloth was still hanging limply.

'He did it all for us,' the elderly stretcher bearer spoke with a heavy burden of guilt. 'A dozen of us stretcher bearers were crowded into a small alley waiting for the chance to move forward. He was behind us. Then all of a sudden, from God knows which rooftop, one of those bastard reactionaries dropped a hand grenade right on top of us. While it was still smoking and rolling around, this comrade shouted to us to duck down, and leapt on top of it, covering it with his body.'

The young woman gave another short scream. I fought back my tears and spoke to the stretcher bearers, sending them on their way. Turning back, I saw that the young bride had already quietly moved an oil lamp to the bedside and had undone his clothing; her recent bashfulness had completely disappeared and she was solemnly and piously washing his body. The tall young courier lay there without uttering a sound.

I suddenly came to my senses and leaping up, stumbled off to fetch the doctor. When the doctor and I hurried up with needle and syringe, the young woman was sitting down facing the bed.

Her head was lowered as stitch by stitch she repaired the hole in the shoulder of his uniform. The doctor listened to the courier's heart, then stood up slowly. 'There's no need to give him an injection.' I went forward and felt his hand: it was icy cold. But the young woman, as if seeing and hearing nothing, continued with her work, finely and closely stitching up the hole. I really couldn't stand the sight of it, and said in a low voice, 'Don't stitch it!' She threw me a peculiar glance, then lowered her head and continued to sew methodically, stitch after stitch. I wanted to pull her away, wanted to break through this cloying atmosphere, wanted to see him sit up, see him bashfully smile. But unwittingly my hand knocked against something next to me. I stretched out my hand to feel it. It was the meal he had left me – two hard, dry, steamed rolls.

A health worker called someone to bring a coffin, and took the quilt from the courier's body ready to place him inside. At this the young woman, her face ashen, seized the quilt from his hands and glaring at him fiercely, laid half of the quilt smoothly over the bottom of the coffin, and folded the remainder to cover the length of the courier's body. The health worker protested awkwardly, 'The quilt . . . was borrowed from the people.'

'It's mine,' she shouted furiously, then wrenched her head away. In the moonlight I saw the tears shining in her eyes. I saw too that wine-coloured quilt with its sprinkling of lilies – the symbols of purity and love – covering the face of that ordinary young man who hauled bamboos.

Translated by R. A. Roberts

SKETCHES FROM THE 'CATTLE SHED'

DING LING

A SHRILL WHISTLE shrieked through the air, resounding along the full length of the corridor and out into the square beyond the windows. The ear-piercing sound rent the curtain of darkness, and the misty, blue light of dawn crept quietly into my prison cell. The naked electric light bulb hanging from the ceiling seemed yellower than ever. My warder, Tao Yun, pushed aside her quilt, climbed down from the brick bed and hurried out of the room, pulling the door shut behind her and fixing the lock firmly. I listened intently. Outside a low rumble of footsteps could be heard moving down the corridor. I listened even more attentively, hoping to detect a light and often rapid footstep, a slight cough and a low, sweet greeting. 'Oh! What are they taking from the end of the corridor? Ah! They are taking brooms. They are going to do a major clean-up and they're going to sweep the square outside my window.' As if a stone had been cast into a tranquil pool, my heart began to pulsate. I dressed quickly and began to pace up and down beside the brick bed. I was waiting for Tao Yun, waiting for her to come back. Maybe they would let me go out and sweep the ground. Even if they would just let me sweep inside the main door beside the stairs and along the corridor I wouldn't mind. Ah! Even if they would just let me sweep those places and not go on to the square, even if my waist was sore and my back ached, even if . . . I could still feel that we were labouring together, and yearning for each other in the midst of our labour, and. . . . Ah! Such extravagant longings! When the crowd of you came back from sweeping the square and I was still in the corridor, we could watch one another surreptitiously, we could gaze at each other, letting our eyes tell how we had missed one another. You would give a tranquil smile of warm sincerity that no one else could detect and, just as thirty years ago, those eyes filled with the freshness of the morning sun would give me boundless encouragement. That dauntless confidence in the future, those unquenchable hopes, that healthy optimism, the strength to defy all difficulties and obstacles. . . . How I longed for that silent, vitalizing support, and, now that I was facing the possibility of mental collapse at any moment, it was a thousand times more necessary, a thousand times more important to me than it had been thirty years ago!

There was no hope. Tao Yun hadn't come back. With a sudden, agile movement, I leaped on to the brick bed, and trembling with fear, stood watching out from behind the window. An old uniform hanging from the upper window frame concealed my face. Through a narrow gap in the cloth I silently combed the square, searching through the crowd of sweepers: here, there, at the front, below my window, group after group. . . . Then, in the early morning light, on the frost-covered square, among the moving crowds, I found in the distance, right in the centre of my window, that figure that seemed small and thin even in its padded cotton clothing, and those large, bright eyes under that thick, heavy fur hat. I lightly pushed aside the uniform that hung at the window and a ray of sunshine shone on to my face. I watched him intently as he raised his great bamboo broom. He – he had seen me. Taking huge paces, he swept rapidly to his right and left, coming in a straight line towards me. Raising his head, he gazed intently at the familiar face partially revealed inside the window. He opened his mouth as if he wanted to speak, as if he was saying something. What audacity! My heart began to pound rapidly and I hastily pulled the uniform back over the window, leaving just a narrow slit to peep through. I wanted him to come closer so that I could have a clearer view of him: was he thinner and older, or fatter and even more rosy-cheeked? I didn't discover whether anyone was shadowing him or whether anyone had noticed me. . . . But suddenly I heard the lock on my door rattle: Tao Yun was about to come in. I thought of ignoring her – it did not intimidate me that she would vent her fury on me – but could I really afford it? I couldn't let her know, must safeguard my secret, my happy secret. Otherwise they would be sure to paint the two upper panes of my window with a thick coating of lime as well, parting me permanently from the bright blue sky, the snow-covered countryside, the thick tangle of tree branches where crows and magpies often came to roost, and that vital, living, outside world of people coming and going. Most of all, I would no longer be able to savour those unspoken words and the boundless feeling in those gazes. So with a movement lighter and quicker than any cat, I slid down into a sitting position on the brick bed, as if I had just wakened from a deep sleep and although I had got dressed, was still reluctant to leave the world of dreams. She opened the door and came in, detecting nothing out of the ordinary. All she said was, 'Get up! Wash your face, rake the stove and sweep the room!'

Thus a false alarm was averted, but my heart was still thumping wildly. I could no longer search for that lost shadow. The siren shrieked again to indicate that early morning stint was over. They would now return to that big room of theirs in preparation for starting their day's labour.

These perilous activities of mine behind the window also brought me a few fleeting seconds of happiness three times a day when the prisoners went *en masse* to collect their meals from the communal kitchen. At every meal they had to line up in a long queue, and after muttering political incantations, confessing their errors and asking for punishment, passed in single file beneath my window on the way to the canteen. After collecting their food they would return in a line to their large 'cattle shed'. Each time Tao Yun left to fetch my food for me (I had no right to fetch my own – probably because they were afraid that I might see somebody, or somebody might see me), I would dodge behind the window, waiting. Tao Yun always walked behind the ranks of the prisoners with a crowd of other warders, so as the inmates went to and fro, I could stand behind my covered window, surreptitiously push aside the old uniform and reveal my face, then, a moment later, once more conceal myself behind the uniform. This way, crafty Tao Yun and the horde of brutal, so-called 'rebel soldiers' were never able to wrest from me those few seconds of rapture that I enjoyed a few times each day. These paltry pleasures supported me through my most difficult years with their days of misery and their long, sleepless nights. What an inspiration they were to my will to live.

LETTERS

Tao Yun had at first been quite sympathetic towards me. At public condemnation meetings, at denunciation parades, and during manual labour, she had found all sorts of ways to give me a little protection. She even acted contrary to the wishes of the multitude by frequently buying me good food and urging me to eat more. I was often deeply moved by these acts of goodwill on her part. But ever since several people had come from Beijing under the signboard of the Military Control Commission, and interrogated me day and night for a month, Tao Yun had shown an intense hatred of me and kept me locked in my small room under heavy surveillance. I was followed closely even when I went to the toilet. She was almost illiterate, yet she would examine at length anything I had written and order me to read it to her. Later she simply confiscated all my paper and my ballpoint pen, and would question me harshly without the slightest provocation. No longer did I see the softer side of her.

I had not a single book and not a single newspaper, and apart from her, I never saw even the shadow of another person inside that tiny room. All I could do was sit blankly like a mute, or pace up and down the floor. How were these endless days and sleepless nights to be endured? Under these circumstances, now when I thought of the tiny seven-metre-square thatched room in our home area where we had once lived – that room that had been raided dozens of times, where we had suffered to the full humiliations and beatings and where I had spent so many days and nights in terror – I was filled with nostalgia for that shining little paradise. Even if we were battered by violent storms, at least the two of us were together! At least it was our home. It was the place where we two sat in silent watch on the small brick bed, where we ate at the tiny table, where we exchanged looks of silent understanding. Two people, hands clasped tightly together, hearts beating together, together coping with the nocturnal visits of those brutal, malignant, destructive hooligans. . . . What precious evenings and deep nights! We supported one another, each drawing strength from the other, dispelled all doubts and suspicions and strengthened our mutual trust. In the midst of difficulties we sought existence, and in our blind alley we sought the road to life. But now I had left all of it. Only evil seeped its way into my lonely soul. A loneliness like death itself was choking the last feeble breath out of me. When would I once more gaze in delight at your radiantly happy face? When would I again hear your deep, strong voice? At present, even if I had a pair of powerful wings, I could not burst out of this cage which imprisoned me so securely. Even if I held the most ardent hopes, I had no way of embracing even a ray of sunshine! All I could do was quietly recite to myself a poem from the days of the underground struggle that we used to like to sing: 'Prisoners, prisoners of the times. We have committed no crime. We are here from the front lines, from the firing line of class struggle. No matter how it is repressed, blood is still boiling. . .'

One day while I was out in the corridor attending to the built-in stove, a shrill whistle rent the air, and out of the large room next door surged a crowd of 'demons and monsters'. As they moved rapidly towards the main door, I gingerly raised my head to watch them, but all I could see were the outlines of a crowd of men with pieces of white cloth pinned to their backs. None of them turned to look at me, and the passageway was very dark, so I could not distinguish one from the other and did not find the figure I was hoping to. But suddenly I felt something fall lightly to the ground beside my foot. I instinctively stood on it, my heart beginning to race. What a wonderful opportunity, Tao Yun was out. I quickly felt it with my fingers: it was a crumpled ball of paper, no larger than one's fingertip. Without stopping to give the matter further thought, I hastily thrust it into my blouse, then sauntered casually into my prison room and slipped it underneath my bedding. Then I quietly returned to the corridor and finished raking the stove. I finished all the tasks I was supposed to do, and calmly and sedately lay down on the bed. But in fact my heart was burning like a fire, that tiny ball of paper underneath me was baking me, burning me. Superficial tranquillity could not conceal the excitement that was churning through my heart. 'Ah, how could you have imagined, how could you have known the frame of mind I have been in lately? You really are a bold one! Don't you know that it's against the rules? I'm really elated, I welcome your audacity! What piddling law is it anyway? We ought to revolt! We have no choice but to do this, we ought to do this. . .'

Shortly afterwards Tao Yun came in. With a grim look on her face she silently inspected the room, but could find nothing in its single table and chair to arouse her slightest suspicions. Seeing my look of exhaustion, she roared, 'Got another headache?' I grunted in the affirmative, at which she stopped observing me, turned and walked out, locking the door behind her. I didn't move. The room was perfectly still and through the two upper panes of my window, two shafts of sunlight shone on to the grey mud floor beyond the brick bed. Tao Yun! There's no need to spy on me through that little hole in the door. I won't let you see anything. I understand you.

Only when I was absolutely certain that I was alone in the room and unobserved did I smooth out that little ball of paper. It was a brightly coloured piece of a cigarette packet. The creased, white inner side of the paper was covered thickly with black speckles that resembled a nest of ants. Only by looking very closely could I recognize them as characters. You are also in a 'cattle shed', living in the eye of the public. How it must have taxed your ingenuity to write this!

He had written: 'You must steadfastly believe in the Party, believe in the masses, believe in yourself and believe in time. History will draw the final conclusion. You must live on! Take a long-term view of things, live for the realization of Communism, live for the sake of our children, live for our future! I love you for ever.'

Almost all the intimate sentiments on the letter had been expressed to me many times before, yet now they seemed so fresh and forceful that I felt as if I were hearing them for the first time. This letter had been sent to me in the face of great peril. In the present circumstances, what else could he have said to me? . . . I was determined to do as the letter exhorted, and do my utmost to make a success of it. He could be reassured of that. It was just that . . . what in fact could I do? Apart from cudgelling my brains all day in this dark little room, what else could I do? All I could do was wait, wait, go out each morning to rake the stove, clean out the cinders and wait to discover another crumpled ball of paper, wait for another ball of paper to land on the ground beside me.

As I'd anticipated, sometimes I would discover a withered maize leaf beside the stove, or perhaps the corner of an old newspaper, or a discarded matchbox. What boundless happiness these ingenious ruses brought me! They were my only spiritual nourishment. They acted as a replacement for newspapers, books and everything that could brighten my room with a little life. They comforted me, encouraged me, brought me hope. I wanted to keep them, keep them for ever; they were poetry, they were fiction, they were eternal keepsakes. Often, when I was certain that no one was watching me, I would pull them out and fondle them, arrange them neatly in order and in a low voice recite them over and over again, or I would lay them at my breast to let them burn like a fire next to my heart. Below are some of those poetic exhortations that I recited so often and which became indelibly printed on my memory.

'They can wrest from you your bodily health, but they cannot deprive you of your healthy mind. You are a white sail on the deep ocean floating far into the distance. Hope lies in your struggle with the waves. I am watching closely as you chart your course, and the earnest hopes of the people are at one with mine.'

'Being locked in a small room isn't so bad, you don't have to hear so many shameless lies; with no one to disturb you, you can become intoxicated with your own memories. Those heroes who once brought you hope of a glorious future, and whom you endowed with life, will achieve frame through your creation, and through them your name will live for ever. In the process of recollection, they will become richer, more mature, while you will attain boundless happiness.'

'Forget the names of those people who harmed you; hold fast to the names of those who stretched out a helping hand in times of difficulty. Don't consider wolves and jackals to be people, and don't be disappointed in mankind because it includes such as they. You must look far ahead to the clouds of dawn; the day will come when they will shine with radiant glory.'

'For you it is a matter of pride never to ask for pity, but there are always many who show great concern for your plight. I am not the only one who silently cries out at the vicissitudes of your life. You belong to the people; you must take good care of yourself.'

'As the dark night passes, the light of dawn approaches. The bitter cold of winter turns to spring. Violent storms cannot beat down a tender stalk of grass, let alone a tall and mighty tree! Your attainments were not charitably bestowed upon you by anyone, nor can they be assassinated, annihilated by the sinister talons of the perverse and violent. Straighten your back; fearlessly live on.'

'We are not alone. Who can say how many talented people who have contributed much to the revolution are now suffering hardship? We are just a drop of water in the ocean, not worth grieving over! Brace yourself, save your energy, prepare for golden opportunities of the future. On no account become pessimistic.'

'. . .'

These brief letters could be collated into a pamphlet, into a small book. I tied them into a roll and carried them like a treasure inside my blouse. They would accompany me through the world to the end of my days.

But alas! That day when I stood in handcuffs, that day when I was stripped naked and given a body search, my only wealth, my cherished poems, were destroyed as pieces of waste paper. All my entreaties that these were evidence of my crimes and must be preserved, came to nothing. Gone were those poems more precious to me than any priceless treasure. Those little pieces of paper that had shared with me long hours of torment had left me for ever. But, even so, those letters were eternally buried in my heart, eternally imprinted on my memory.

PARTING

The spring winds blew a green veil over the plains of the Great Northern Wilderness. The weather grew warmer day by day and, according to the season, the spring sowing had already started. The inhabitants of these large and small rooms of ours diminished in number daily. I heard that some people had already gone home to return to their former work units, while others had been assigned to labour in production brigades. New hope sprang into everyone's heart.

———

On 14 May, just after breakfast, a uniformed man came to my room, and I sensed that a new chapter in my destiny was about to begin. I fervently hoped that I might be able to return to that seven-metre-square thatched room where we had once found the warmth of home. I fondly imagined that we might once more live the pitiful yet happy life of a couple of industrious, impoverished peasants.

I politely sat at one end of the brick bed, and invited the visitor to take a seat in the centre. He looked me up and down for a moment, and then asked, 'How old are you?'

'Sixty-five,' I answered.

He asked further, 'You seem to be in good shape, can you do manual labour?'

'I've always done manual labour,' I replied.

'We intend to let you go and do manual labour. We think it will be better for you.'

I didn't understand what he was getting at, so I made no reply.

'We're sending you to XX Brigade to work. You will be under the "dictatorship of the revolutionary masses", do you understand?'

My heart lurched. XX Brigade, I understood only too well. I could expect no gentle treatment at that place. I had already had some experience of a few of the people there. Group after group of people from XX Brigade had been to my home in the depths of the night; there was nothing they hadn't done. Yet I was not concerned: every place had a certain number of scoundrels, and would certainly also have good people. Furthermore, good people were always in the majority. I simply asked, 'When do I leave?'

'Straight away.'

'I'd like to sort out a change of clothes for the summer, may I go home first?' I was thinking of my little thatched room again. I'd been away from it for almost ten months and I'd heard that one night during the winter, someone had broken in through the window. Heaven only knew what state the empty room was in now.

'We'll send someone to collect them for you and have them sent to XX Brigade.' He stood up as if he were about to leave.

I said hastily, 'I'd like to request a meeting with C. There are a few things we must talk about. We have our household responsibilities.'

As I spoke, I stood up and moved towards the door as if I wouldn't let him go until he had assented.

He muttered something to himself and surveyed me for a moment, then agreed to my request. I let him through the door and he went out closing it behind him.

How could they still refuse to let us go home? Why would they still not allow us to be together? After all, what crime had we committed? Since July last year when I had been seized from the poultry farm where I had been working and imprisoned here, I had been through beatings, denunciations and interrogations. Hadn't the two factions of the farm already formed an alliance? I'd heard that now they were running along the right track again, so why was there no end to this treatment of us? It was really incomprehensible!

In fact, C. and I had been separated since July last year when I had begun my solitary confinement in this little room. Only in October when this 'prison in disguise' was enlarged to accommodate a great influx of people, did C. come to live in the large 'cattle shed' next door to mine. Even though we were not permitted to speak to each other, we were at least living under the same roof and still met by chance occasionally. Sometimes we could even gaze at one another through the window, not to mention the fact that for the last few months I'd been receiving his brief, illegal letters. But now it seemed that even this life of bitter, mutual longing was to become the subject of nostalgic thoughts and sweet memories. I would go alone to XX Brigade, to a 'tiger' brigade, to subject myself to the 'dictatorship of the revolutionary masses'. But where would he be sent? When would we see one another again? With a single blow, my life was about to be cut off from all joy, solicitude, comfort and the faintest gleam of brightness. All that would be left me was suffering, exhaustion, anger, yearning and disappointment. . . . I would have to fight those accursed devils. I must never surrender to them, never allow myself to be dragged down. Dying was relatively easy, it was living that was so difficult. Death would be quite comfortable, yet living was so painful! But I was a member of the Communist Party (even though I had been expelled from the Party at the end of 1957, over eleven years ago, I still considered myself a member, made demands on myself as one and regarded everything from the point of view of a Party member). All I could do was continue to tread this endless path beset with hardships and danger. In the face of death I must always seek life!

The door opened with a creak and C. walked in. The whole world took on a different look. Sunlight filled this tiny, dark prison cell. Understanding the preciousness of time, I rushed forward and grasped those firm, outstretched hands, gazed into that face it seemed I hadn't seen for decades. His expression betrayed a complexity of emotions: he was overjoyed at seeing me, yet agonized by our imminent separation. He wanted to encourage me to stand up to even greater trials, yet was worried by my thin, pallid face and white temples; he wanted to be gentle, but did not dare to dissolve the little courage I still possessed by his kindness; he wanted to embrace me fervently, but was afraid to trigger the release of uncontrollable emotions. We gazed at one another in silence, unable to prevent the hot tears stinging our eyelids, but suppressing them with a shake of the head and a forced bitter smile. He nodded and said in a low voice, 'I know.'

'Where will you be going?' I asked quietly.

'I still don't know,' he shook his head.

He pulled a banknote from his pocket and lightly and discreetly placed it in my hand, I knew that this was his entire five *yuan* savings from his monthly living allowance of fifteen *yuan*, but I had no choice but to accept it. I only had a little over one *yuan* in my pocket.

He said, 'Don't hesitate to use it. Don't skimp yourself on food and don't eat too badly. You mustn't let yourself collapse physically. It won't be long before I find some way to. . .'

I said that I wanted to go home to pick up some clothes.

He said dejectedly, 'Someone else has already moved in. Don't bother about that place any more. I'll go and sort out your clothes and have the things you need sent to you. Don't you worry about it. I'll write to you every month. If there's anything you need, I'll find some way of getting it to you.'

I choked on my words, forcing back all those things I wanted to say most. And the words he most wanted to say, I could only read in his eyes. Our hands were locked tightly together, our eyes riveted on one another in a gaze that neither of us could break. We were facing immediate separation. Without even a reunion, we were once more to be torn apart. And who could know whether we would ever meet again?

Crash! The door was suddenly kicked open by a leather-booted foot, and a young man glared into the room.

'What do you want?' I asked.

'What do I want! It's getting late. Get your things and come straight away!'

He was obviously the 'escort' sent from XX Brigade to fetch me. Whether he was Dong Chao or Xue Ba* made no difference, I now had to set off for the 'forage farm' and a life of manual labour.

C. helped me to roll up my thin quilt and the grey cotton-padded mattress that had been issued to me by the Huabei Bureau in Zhangjiakou at the time of the victory over the Japanese. To make things easier for me, C. tied them and my extra clothing into two rolls, so that I could carry one on my back and one in front of me.

That done, he hesitated for a few moments, then said resolutely, 'I'd better go. Take care of yourself, keep calm and if you run into problems, don't let them upset you. Even if you hear bad news, like . . . oh, nothing. All in all, you must prepare for all eventualities, especially bad ones. In any case, there's nothing to be afraid of, considering the situation we're already in, what else is there to be afraid of? I'm just worried that you. . .'

His words struck me dumb with fear. I realized there was something he had been hiding from me that he now had no choice but to make me prepare for mentally. Ah! Just what was the bad news that he was keeping from me?

Seeing my stupefied, tear-filled eyes, he comforted me, saying, 'Nothing has happened, it's just me being over-cautious. I'm afraid that if something unexpected happens you won't be able to take it in your stride. In short, this will all come to an end eventually. We must believe in ourselves. The situation isn't limited to just the two of us. Maybe it won't be long before everything changes. We must prepare to welcome back the good times when they come. It won't do to endure the hard times but not last out for the happy times afterwards.' He sought to bring a smile to my face with his optimistic words, but I was already incapable of smiling. This ominous parting had already crushed my heart into fragments.

* Dong Chao and Xue Ba: two gaolers under whose guard one of the heroes in the Chinese classical novel *Outlaws of the Marsh*, Lin Chong, was exiled.

He left the room before me. I gathered up my belongings and followed my 'escort' from that tiny room out into the square. The spring wind stroked my body, and in the distance, I could see a figure standing by a well under a scholar tree, waving his hand in my direction. He was drawing water for the boiler room. His arm was raised high, as if in carefree, joyous, warm farewell to a friend setting out on a journey to distant parts.

March 1979, written in Youyi Hospital
Translated by R. A. Roberts

THE RIGHT
TO LOVE

ZHANG KANGKANG

1

IN THIS COLD northern city, summer always seems to be late. Not until July, when the Persian chrysanthemum is in full blossom, are the banks of the Songhua River shaded by the leafy branches of willows. Although this was the second summer after what people considered to be their second liberation, not everyone could feel that summer was really approaching.

A girl of twenty-seven or twenty-eight walked slowly down the gangplank of the passenger steamer that had just arrived from the lower reaches of the river, and continued, seemingly aimlessly, along the river bank. She was wearing the most ordinary of checked, long-sleeved blouses and cotton-polyester trousers without sharp creases. Her short, slightly auburn hair, carelessly braided into two short plaits, hung at her shoulders. As she walked slowly, gazing at the gorgeous summer colours of the banks of the Songhua River that had suddenly come into view, her large, yet detached and indifferent eyes seemed to register a slight surprise. Even her small lips, usually pressed firmly together in a serious expression, now parted a little in astonishment.

A small white motorboat skimmed like a bird across the surface of the river before her, the happy laughter of a crowd of young people splashing through the air with each jet of spray. A ferry full of holiday-makers was steaming towards Sunshine Island on the northern side of the river. A young man in sunglasses standing in the stern was waving his white sunhat at someone on the bank. Snatches of songs and music floated up to her from the water, and following the sound with her eyes, she saw several small sampans floating down the river. On one boat, a girl in a dripping-wet bathing suit was playing a guitar while several other girls, shading themselves with red nylon umbrellas, listened quietly. On another boat, a girl was playing an accordion while several young men merrily nodded their heads to mark time and sang along.

On the embankment beside her, crowds of people surged back and forth. There were all sorts of people: some carrying swimming costumes, some carrying bread and bottles of beer, some with cameras slung around their necks. The girls were wearing brightly coloured, short skirts in novel styles, and she could even see sleeveless dresses and cheongsams that for so many years no one had dared to wear. There were skirts with frilled borders, bodices embroidered at the breast with flowers of golden thread.

She was stunned. She had just arrived from a hospital on a remote commune on the lower reaches of the river and had not been home for about a year. Never in her wildest dreams could she have imagined that Stalin Park on the riverbank would have undergone such a startling change. Guitars, dresses, sunhats were things that only appeared in hazy memories of her childhood, but now even the waterside club with its pointed Russian-style roof that twelve years ago had been denounced as 'typical revisionist architecture' had been newly painted, and raised its head proudly amongst the dancing willows on the embankment.

She rubbed her eyes and felt a wave of exhaustion sweep over her feeble body. Her head was aching as if it would split. She was just about to look for a bench where she could sit and rest for a while, when her attention was caught by a sudden burst of applause that erupted a little way in front of her.

From beneath a brilliantly coloured Youth League flag that hung on a sturdy willow tree nearby, the drawn-out notes of a violin reached her from the midst of a dense crowd of onlookers. She quickly recognized the bold, graceful melody of Sarasate's violin solo 'Andalusian Romance'. She was all too familiar with that tune – its joyful, leaping strains seeped into her despondent heart like rays of sunshine evoking memories of her childhood and bygone happy days with her family. She had not heard that melody for years, but it had once been one of her father's favourite violin solos. She rested her head against the tree trunk behind her and half closed her eyes, immersing herself body and soul in the music. What astonished her was the unexpectedly rich feeling that the violinist infused into his music. She felt that his smooth, skilful technique and his original approach to each passage arose from his unique understanding of the piece. As she listened, she felt herself drawn into the rhythm of the music and couldn't prevent herself from starting to hum along with it.

Suddenly she involuntarily covered her mouth with her hand, and raising her head in terror looked around her. Only when she realized that no one was paying any attention to her did the wild beating of her heart subside. She stood entranced for a long while, listening attentively to the notes that came flying out from the centre of the crowd, then suddenly seemed to awake from her reverie and flurriedly stood on tiptoe, peering into the centre of the circle of onlookers as if trying to make out the face of the violinist. But this was a Sunday and there were simply too many people in the way so, disregarding all else, she began to squeeze her way through the crowd, elbowing aside the enraptured audience without even caring whether she trod on people's toes or not. Finally, her face bathed in perspiration, she pushed her way to the front. She pulled herself together and looked into the empty space in the centre of the crowd where the violinist was continuing his impassioned performance. An involuntary 'Ah!' escaped from her lips, and she stood there like a simpleton, struck dumb with terror.

He, a young man of twenty-two or twenty-three, was completely engrossed in the exquisite sounds of his own music. His large, fiery eyes glittered with enthusiasm, his high-bridged nose twitched forcefully and his largish mouth hung slightly open in a buoyant grin that was oblivious to his surroundings. A lock of curly black hair hanging down over his wide forehead and giving him a Bohemian air moved rapidly up and down with the rhythm of the music. His body swayed joyfully and he tapped a lively beat on the ground with one foot. The high-spirited melody gushed from the white strings of his bow like a surging waterfall. His face was the embodiment of joy and even his eyebrows seemed to be laughing. If he could have, he would have simply taken the violin in his arms and begun to dance.

'Spanish. . . ,' she muttered numbly, her eyes fixed on the gleaming violin in his hands. Her face turned deathly pale and cold sweat poured from her forehead. The air seemed to have become parched and stifled her breathing, her head reeled as waves of nausea swept over her. Even the trees seemed to be swaying around her. She became vaguely conscious that she was suffering a relapse of her illness, and in terror tried to grasp something to steady herself, but she was surrounded by people. The crowd suddenly broke into applause and the young man bowed calmly, apparently preparing to accept their warm invitation to perform another piece.

Gold stars flashed before her eyes, the image of the young man became indistinct and seemed to change into that of a white-haired old man with a violin hung around his neck, standing with shoulders bowed on a high platform, undergoing denunciation.

'Xiao Mo, you're crazy!' A shrill cry escaped from her throat, she seemed to be trying to say something, but her legs collapsed and she fell to the ground.

Hearing that heart-rending cry, the violinist suddenly turned his head and, seeing her, stood rooted to the spot for a moment. Then he leapt towards her with a shout:

'Sister!. . .'

2

The girl was named Shu Bei and nicknamed Beini. Her father, who had been dead for over two years, had been the head of the arts department and a professor of music in one of the city's universities. At one time he had taken great pride in sharing a surname with Schubert, and people respectfully addressed him as 'Shu Bo'. Because of his passionate love of music, he had chosen a character from the Chinese transliteration of Beethoven for his daughter's name and one from that of Mozart for his son Shu Mo. His daughter had once had as sweet a voice as her mother who had been deputy director of an opera troupe, but since her mother had died uncleared of a false charge twelve years ago, wiping the sound of her own voice from the world, Shu Bei had rarely sung again. Now she was almost without family. Her only relative was a beloved younger brother who worked in an electrical machinery factory.

When she regained consciousness, she found herself lying in bed in a dazzling white hospital ward. Her headache seemed to have eased considerably but she still felt a little nauseous. Thinking back on her sudden fainting fit, she could not repress a bitter smile: the same thing had happened so many times before that the head of the commune hospital had urged her to come back to have a thorough check-up and undergo treatment. But in fact she herself was well aware of the cause of the trouble. Since the autumn and winter of 1974 when that overwhelming disaster had struck, headaches and dizziness had become a common occurrence. Today on the riverbank she had been totally unprepared for the discovery that her brother had gone so far as to break their long-standing tacit agreement and had begun to play the violin again. And that he should perform European folk tunes in a public place was beyond anything she could have imagined.

She opened her eyes and saw Shu Mo sitting motionless at her bedside closely watching the speed at which the liquid was moving through the drip that hung at the head of her bed. On top of a cupboard next to the bed lay an old, but painstakingly repaired violin case.

As if catching sight of something terrifying, she rapidly looked away from the violin case and said in a low voice, 'Take it away.'

Shu Mo hesitated for a moment as if wanting to defend himself, but then obediently picked it up and slid it under the bed.

She nodded her head, signalling to her brother to pass her the satchel that she always carried with her, and with one hand pulled out a white envelope and handed it to him. Her hand trembled violently and her expression, which had just begun to show some vitality, once more became sombre.

'Read it, Xiao Mo, you must have forgotten it,' she said in a tone that brooked no discussion.

Shu Mo swallowed, and flushing scarlet looked at his sister with beseeching eyes. But it was no use. He knew his sister's temperament. But to read a thing like this at a time like this seemed quite unnecessary to him – even though his father's deathbed wish had once occupied a commanding place in his heart.

He cautiously ascertained that the other patients were paying no attention to them, then in an indistinct voice began to read it aloud. Papa – they had once had such a warm and forthright father, so full of vitality. On bright, clear summer days he would take brother and sister to the Songhua River to swim, and there on the jade-white beach would play his violin, letting the music flow with the river into the faraway sea. He would always attract a large audience, yet remain totally unaware of it. Every Sunday their house would be filled with students come to 'catch up on missed lessons', but as soon as the first notes of their father's violin sounded, not even the sound of breathing could be heard in the room. The music transported everyone to a primeval forest under deep snow where a nimble fawn bounded. From beneath the snow leapt the clear, lively water of a warm spring chattering interminably . . . ting, ting . . . ting, ting . . . the sound of the violin stopped abruptly, and suddenly the room overflowed with uninhibited laughter. Everyone became as lively as a concert keyboard.

But since their father had returned home after two years in the 'cattleshed' (his crime had been to write several patriotic songs during the War of Resistance Against Japan) and found that his wife had departed this world over a year before, he had become taciturn, sorrowful and desolate. Only when he saw his violin would a light gleam in his eyes. He spent almost all his spare time playing that violin. Their mother had brought it back from overseas for him and it had escaped destruction on the day the house was raided because, by coincidence, Shu Mo had taken it out with him. Sometimes Papa would spend all day playing the violin, and pitiful as it was, though he could only play simple exercise pieces, he never grew tired of them and would play them dozens of times in succession without a break. This made Shu Mo think: there is no way to prevent a person loving what he loves. Papa often liked to say, 'You children understand that music is the sunshine of life.'

That was how deeply he loved music, right up until a moment before he died. It was January of that bitter winter of '76. Everyone was still immersed in deepest grief, yet the university, amidst the chanting of the slogan, 'the direction of revolution in education must not be subverted', began to hold a series of denunciation meetings. The first on the list for condemnation was none other than Shu Bo. That day he was notified that he would never again be permitted to teach. He had already become aged and feeble and was now no more than a guttering candle struggling to emit its last flicker of light. How could he sustain this mortal blow? Shu Mo supported him home. 'Violin, violin. . .' the old man mumbled the word over and over again, then suddenly struggled up out of his reclining chair, seized the violin that had accompanied him through several decades of life and stumbled out of the door before brother and sister could prevent him. He sank down on the balcony railing and hurled the violin from their fourth-storey apartment down into the street far below.

Shu Mo glanced quietly at the sheet of white paper in his hand and anguish crept into his heart. On that dimly moonlit night, when the sound of the violin smashing on the ground below reached their ears, their father lost consciousness. Just before he died, he had gazed at the two sobbing children and attempted to speak: 'Mo, you mustn't study the violin any more . . . Beini, when you marry, you should choose a worker . . . be an . . . ordinary person . . . whatever you do, don't . . . get involved in politics . . . don't love. . .!'

'Don't love. . .' the old man seemed to have something constricting his throat, he gestured with an effort, but could not make a sound.

He finally closed his eyes. Amid the soughing of the winter wind, only a lonely lamp kept the two children company, no one dared to visit them. Only the soundless lament of the broken-stringed violin on the snowy ground outside bade farewell to that pure soul. Shu Bei, who understood, recorded her father's last words with a trembling hand, and from then on carried them concealed about her person.

Their father had left the world nursing such indignation and injustice that he had even forbidden his son, whom he had brought up so carefully, to continue with music. His love, his ideals had been smashed along with his beloved violin. Everything was over. When he expired, he seemed full of hatred. 'Don't love'; don't love what? Don't love those things that their parents once loved? Shu Mo, waking in the depths of the night from torturous nightmares, often felt perplexed. He could not believe that a man, who had loved life as his father had, could leave behind such a despairing dying wish. From the time when he had first begun to comprehend the world, his father had tirelessly instructed him to love the Party, love the people and love his work. Thus, since he was small, 'love' had taken root in his heart as a sacred and unshakable belief. He found it difficult to imagine how someone who had no love of life could continue to live.

But afterwards he very quickly unravelled this skein of doubt and sincerely forgave his father – for the old man could not have imagined that six months after his death China would undergo such an immense transformation. If he had lived to see the smashing of the Gang of Four, would he have left behind such a heart-broken dying wish? Shu Mo spent many a sleepless night in those jubilant days, tossing and turning in his bed, pondering this problem, and finally became convinced that he was right. His mind at rest, the first thing he did was to use his savings to buy a new violin and place it in the old case that had lain empty for so long. He began to practise in secret. He sounded out his sister, hoping to gain her support, but Shu Bei remained scrupulously faithful to every word of her father's instructions.

'I've always been afraid that you wouldn't do as Papa instructed,' Shu Bei said listlessly, 'and by the look of things I was right. You see things too simplistically. Do you think that Papa's words only applied to that time? They didn't, he was thinking about our whole lives. He may have spoken only a few short sentences, but they contained a lesson that he sacrified his life for. The main reason you don't take his words seriously is because you can't bear to part with your violin, you love it too much.'

'Um, perhaps so . . . I do love it,' Shu Mo candidly admitted, surprising even himself. He seemed to have intended to bluff his way through as he had always done before, but found himself unable to do so. He glanced rapidly out of the window, then mischievously blinking his eyes whispered in Shu Bei's ear, 'Look who's coming – Li Xin. I phoned him and told him you were here.' He hesitated for a moment then went on, 'Do you mean to tell me that you don't love him? You must have had his letter. Maybe today both of us will go against father's dying wish. . .'

Shu Bei's startled eyes opened wide. Through the white curtains she saw the silhouette of a young man pacing up and down the corridor. That tall, thin figure, those high cheekbones that seemed to bespeak of one who knew his own mind, and those thick, wide-rimmed glasses, were all familiar to her. It really was him, him. . .

3

The quiet hospital ward, the spotless white sheets and curtains seemed purposely to draw her back to events of the past. Not long after father had died, and before that bitter winter had passed, Shu Mo developed peritonitis and had to undergo surgery in hospital. Shu Bei had hurried home to look after him. It was in just this kind of hospital ward that she had first come to know that tall, thin, dark young man with eyes that shone with warmth and intelligence. He was in hospital recovering from an accident at work. When he had been brought into the ward in his tattered grass-green cotton-padded clothes and boots padded with reeds, she had mistaken him for a peasant from the suburbs. But the following day she had noticed several books under his pillow. This immediately aroused Shu Mo's intense interest and several days later he told Shu Bei that his fellow patient was a second-year higher middle school intellectual youth from Shanghai called Li Xin. He was now leader of a team of tilers at a farm. A few days later he told Shu Bei that he and this young man held very similar points of view. Because Shu Bei was a nurse, she took on the responsibility of looking after Li Xin, as well as caring for her brother. She did everything quickly and efficiently, and Li Xin silently allowed her to attend to him, just thanking her with a grateful smile. He was not a good talker, especially with girls, but sometimes when she read the newspaper aloud to everyone in the ward, he would continually interrupt her with jokes which kept the other patients in fits of laughter. Shu Mo said he was a humourist. His foot gradually healed until he was able to walk again. One day while he was out, Shu Bei tidied his bed for him, and out of curiosity flipped through some books that had slid out from under his pillow. She started involuntarily: there was Rousseau's *On the Origin and Basis of the Inequality of Man*, Voltaire's *Philosophical Correspondence*, Belinsky's *Literary Illusions* and something called *Selected Writings of Babeuf*. Where did he get these books from? Her heart was still beating wildly when he came in.

'Hey, are you going to take the exams for university?' she asked.

He smiled faintly. 'No, I'm just doing some reading.' He thought for a moment, then added, 'You don't need to take exams to get into university these days. On the contrary, by reading a few books you destroy your qualifications for getting in.'

She didn't question him further; she knew what he was getting at. Later she found out from Shu Mo that the people on his farm had recommended him for university several times, but because he had not been willing to send gifts to the leading cadres, he had been denounced for having 'impure motives for entering college' and had failed to be selected. But he had no regrets. Shu Bei was deeply moved by his story, and unconsciously began to feel new respect and sympathy for him. From then on a tall, thin image grew clearer and brighter in her mind with each passing day. By the time Li Xin was discharged from hospital, he and Shu Mo had already become close friends. Shu Mo invited him to visit their home, and he gladly accepted. He arrived just at the wrong moment, when Shu Bei was washing the dinner dishes and softly singing to herself. By coincidence, she was singing 'Little Track', a popular Russian folksong from the Second World War. As her clear voice enunciated the words 'follow my lover on to the battlefield', he walked in.

Shu Bei blushed scarlet. She didn't like other people to hear her singing, because she was not singing for happiness.

' "Little Track"!' Li Xin cried excitedly, 'I haven't heard that for ages.'

She had never imagined that he would be both familiar with the tune and fond of it. She deliberately put on a stern expression and said, 'Going by little tracks and not treading the broad road – isn't that revisionism!'

'No,' he refuted her in all seriousness, 'I like little tracks! Marx said that only those who toil unceasingly on little rugged mountain tracks have hope of reaching the glorious summit. If everyone walked the flat, safe, broad road, I'm afraid there would be no progress in this world.'

'We don't dare,' Shu Bei poked out her tongue, ' "Little Track" is only for singing inside the house. . .'

He frowned and shook his head self-confidently: 'No, I'm sure this sort of phenomenon can't last for long. Once everyone enters the battlefield the situation will change.'

He walked over to the bookcase, took down the dusty violin case and stood examining it closely. Shu Mo must have already told him its story. Wiping off the thick dust, he said angrily, 'If the violin were not gone, Xiao Mo could play an accompaniment while we sang some songs. This empty violin case is testimony to a crime. It is evidence of those people persecuting artists and destroying culture!'

Shu Bei was terrified. This was the first time she had heard anyone give such an interpretation of the violin case. She looked intently at his thin face, astounded that such a gentle, refined man could say something so passionate and impetuous. What kind of wild stallion of thought raced beneath that placid exterior? Her eyes flashed with admiration. That night he talked with Shu Mo into the early hours, and for the first time his words flowed in an eloquent, ceaseless stream. He described himself as a 'heretic', then roared with laughter. . .

Just before the arrival of spring, he went back to Shanghai to visit his family. Those were the stormy, restless days of April 1976. In May he returned via Harbin, and dropped in to see them before changing trains. He drew a package from his breast and handed it to Shu Mo.

'Keep this safe for me, I trust you.'

Nothing in his flashing eyes gave any hint of trouble looming ahead, yet his heavy frown gave Shu Bei a presentiment that something was about to happen. He left, taking her heart with him.

Shu Mo opened the package and found a thick wad of manuscripts with titles like: 'Who are the real upstarts?', 'Down with the new nobility!', 'Democracy must not be tarnished'. Shu Mo almost danced for joy, shouting his approval, but Shu Bei broke out in a cold sweat. She spent all night considering the matter and finally concealed the manuscripts in a sack of fried flour which she took back to the commune hospital and put inside her pillow. In those endless days, that pillow became her faithful companion, she soaked it with her tears and confided her longings to it. In her eyes that wad of manuscripts was a glowing brick, yet pillowing her head upon it made her feel secure and at peace. In the depths of the silent night, she would even have intimate conversations with it. At first she had tried hard to drive the image of the owner from her mind, but she had found this impossible.

The fragrant linden trees outside the hospital gate were in full flower, and in the early morning before the dew had dried, and again when the magnificent twilight clouds glowed in the sky, she would often stand motionless beneath them, gazing fixedly into the distance. Who was she waiting for, someone asked her. She flushed scarlet. Was she waiting for him, she asked herself. No, no, why should she wait for him? Could she possibly be . . . The thought filled her with confusion. The linden flowers withered, the leaves on the oak trees turned red, but there was no news of him.

Winter departed and spring arrived, the Songhua River thawed and the countryside returned to life. Six months after the fall of the Gang of Four there was still no sign of Li Xin. Then one day in July when the Persian chrysanthemums were in full bloom, Shu Bei suddenly received a long-distance phone call from Shu Mo to say that Li Xin was in Harbin and wanted her to bring the manuscripts back with all possible speed. Only when she had hurried back home did she learn that after returning to the farm he had been placed in isolation on written orders from Beijing and Shanghai for writing a letter to *Red Flag* and supporting the 5 April activities in Nanjing the previous year. He had now been released, but his case had still not been completely cleared, so he had come to Harbin to appeal for help from the provincial Party committee.

Shu Bei gazed at him with soft gentleness, unable to believe her eyes. She asked him in amazement, 'How have you managed to put on weight? I thought. . .'

Li Xin burst out laughing. 'As soon as I heard that the Gang of Four had been crushed, I ate six maize rolls in a single meal, I remained locked up, but it was like living in a sanitorium – the longer I stayed there the fatter I got.'

This sort of laughter was infectious and Shu Bei couldn't help joining in, her heart melting within her. She caught sight of her laughing face in the mirror and suddenly for the first time felt that when she laughed she was still beautiful. It was just that she didn't like to laugh.

To celebrate their reunion, Shu Mo proposed that they sing a song, and took out his violin. Li Xin did not refuse, but began to sing 'Little Track' in a mellow baritone: 'Little track so narrow, o'er the wide plains twists, leading to the distant hills veiled in hazy mists. . .' Shu Bei had never known that he had such a pleasant voice. She longed to join in and sing with him, but she checked herself. As he sang 'I want to travel that long, narrow track, follow my lover on to the battlefield', their eyes met in a glance of deep affection. She felt as if an electric shock had run through her body and in the midst of her panic, as her thoughts turned to love, she realized it was something she had been avoiding for years. Unwilling to admit her feelings, she hastily fled back to the commune hospital.

But perhaps this was a fate that could not be escaped. As the summer of the second year approached – that was not long ago – she had received a letter from Li Xin telling her that he had passed the university entrance exams and been accepted into the philosophy department of Song Jiang University. But far from making Shu Bei excited, this news hit her like a pail of cold water soaking her from head to toe. In the last ten years, words like 'politics' and 'philosophy' had made her feel she was confronting a deadly enemy, and even the fall of the Gang of Four had not made her change her attitude completely. What made her even more distraught was that in this letter, Li Xin had for the first time expressed the love that he had hidden in his heart for the past two years. He said he liked her serene, reserved personality and that, though she was a little too melancholy, she matched perfectly his serious, philosophical temperament.

His letter raised such a tempest in her heart that for several nights she could not sleep a wink. Hadn't she been yearning for love for a long time past? But now that it had come . . . Yes, she did appear depressed and joyless to others, hers was a personality that had been ground out from a life fraught with setbacks and difficulties. A dozen or so years ago, what splendid ideals and enthusiasm for life had filled her childish heart! Every evening, the polished lid of the piano her mother was playing would reflect a round-faced, large-eyed little girl. Mama would affectionately nod her head towards her, and, copying her mother's style, Shu Bei would incline her head slightly and begin to sing in her clear, expressive voice . . . but afterwards everything had changed. Her mother's sudden death and the repeated denunciations that her father suffered had cast a heavy shadow over her heart. She had gone to the countryside and, for no other reason than humming a line of a tune from 'A Visitor to Bing Mountain' on the way back from work one day, she had been reported and denounced at large and small meetings for two weeks. Another time, just because she had worn an old skirt her mother had left her, she had been 'exposed', and ordered to make a self-criticism. She had always been serious in speech and manner and never bothered with minor social conventions, but liked to live her life in her own way, exuding something of the romantic flavour of a musician's family. But everyone found fault with her, regarding her as a 'capitalist' type, and no matter how much hardship she stood or how assiduously she worked, she was never praised for it. Gradually her heart turned cold and she became indifferent to everything. Then on top of it all, in the autumn of '74 something had happened to deal her the heavy blow from which she had never recovered.

There had been a youth from Harbin in the same brigade as her who had pursued her keenly from the start. He would often help her with her work and, if she were bullied, he would step forward and speak out on the side of justice. With the passing of time Shu Bei became very favourably disposed towards him. In the midst of her difficulties he was the only one she could talk to. They showed solicitude for one another and cared for each other. If this is what pure feelings are built on, then the seeds of Shu Bei's first love began to sprout. They fell deeply in love and trusted one another completely. If things could have gone on like that they could have enjoyed a kind of happiness. But suddenly a unit in the city came looking for workers. They both put their names down but, while he was accepted without a hitch and left, she was rejected because of her family problems and had to remain behind. He never wrote her a single letter. In the cold autumn as the leaves fell and the wild geese winged southwards, her heart became encrusted in a thick layer of dawn frost. When she returned to Harbin for New Year, she trudged through the snow to visit him, but the hypocritical smiles on his family's faces made her shiver. He didn't dare to look her straight in the eyes and when he saw her to the door told her with tears in his eyes, 'My family won't agree to it. They say that your family background will prevent you from getting anywhere in life. My organization at work is interfering too and have forbidden me to have any contact with you. There's just nothing I can do.'

At that moment she had truly hoped that the snow piled on the roof might suddenly collapse in an avalanche and bury her. She stood there dumbly like a lonely icicle under the eaves until the bone-chilling winter wind brought her to her senses. Then she ran through the snow-covered streets straight to the opera house where her mother had worked. She wanted to ask just what crime it was that her mother had committed. Hadn't the so-called cases of 'spying for foreign countries' been overturned two years ago and the accused rehabilitated? Wasn't she the equal of that young man? But why was it that he now had the necessary qualifications whilst she did not? She ran into the opera house, but found herself at a complete loss. Confronted by those 'leaders' yawning lazily in their swivel chairs, she couldn't speak a word. Their reply was not a reply, but a warning to her not to try to reverse a correct verdict against someone who had alienated herself from the people.

The young man who had once given her a little happiness and help had left her. She knew that had not been his original intention. She and he were both weaklings unable to withstand the pressure of public opinion. She didn't hate him, but hated . . . Whom did she hate? She didn't dare to tell her father, who was still alive then, nor her innocent brother, for fear of upsetting them. After returning to the brigade, she had fallen seriously ill. (It was then that a good-hearted hospital director had contrived a way to have her transferred to the commune hospital as a nurse.) She had pledged an oath that from then on she would remain on the remote commune for the rest of her life. Although it was partly done in a fit of pique, it also embodied her aspirations. But she had never imagined that love could be independent of human willpower, and that three years later, Li Xin would quietly force his way into her heart. Faced with replying to the expectant Li Xin, she thought of her father's dying wish and felt her answer was predetermined, though still a painful one. She had known that, when she came back to recuperate this time, she would have to make a choice, but had never imagined that he would come so soon . . . spotless white sheets and curtains . . . When they had first got to know one another hadn't their positions been exactly reversed? Then it had been she who each morning had lined up to buy steaming soya bean milk and carried it to his bedside.

'Li Xin has recently been thinking of writing a dissertation called "From 4 May to 5 April".' Shu Mo gently interrupted her meditations, as if urging her to invite him in.

Shu Bei shook her head resolutely. 'My head aches terribly. I'd like to sleep for a while. Go and tell the doctor that while I'm here I'd like to have an EEG done, there's an introductory letter in my bag from the commune hospital.'

Shu Mo walked out pouting angrily.

————

After that, every day at about 6 o'clock, a tall, thin figure silhouetted against the magnificent clouds of the summer evening would lightly pass the window and enter the staff office. A few moments later it would cross the window again and disappear into the dusk. His steps seemed to falter at the door of the ward, but he never came in. 'What's his connection with you? He comes every day to look at your medical records, and the way he minutely examines every detail. . .' The nurses' witticisms brought a pink flush to Shu Bei's face. At such times she longed for her stay in hospital to be extended indefinitely, as if only in the hospital ward could she avert the inevitable talk that loomed ahead of her.

4

But she nevertheless finally came out of hospital. After she had been there for a week, the doctor sent a diagnosis of her electro-encephalogram saying that her headaches were of nervous origin and could be treated with drugs and physiotherapy at the outpatients clinic. She herself felt in better spirits too. Shu Mo pushed her home on the back of his bicycle.

On the way, Shu Mo enthusiastically told her everything that had recently happened at his factory: a certain technician had been promoted to engineer; the workers in a certain workshop had successfully carried out technological reform and received bonuses; some workers had demanded to elect their own workshop foreman. Unexpectedly there was a piece of particularly important news: a couple of lovers who had waited eight years because the administration had refused to approve their marriage had finally been given approval. And the only reason that approval had been withheld before was because the man's father had had a suspect political record while the woman was a Party member. By the look of it, Shu Mo was avidly interested in this news. Not only did he relate in detail many minor incidents that had occured in those eight years of waiting, but he clearly and logically analysed the basis of their mutual love. Shu Bei listened in silence, outwardly preserving her usual cold indifference, but inwardly suppressing violently churning emotions. The story stirred up things that had been constantly on her mind, and added misgivings to the astonishment she had felt in the last few days at the rapid changes that were taking place in society. It wasn't that she was one of those people who show no concern for politics; she had long ago discovered in the newspapers many things she had been yearning to see. Those fresh, daring reports and articles had for a time roused her and moved her to the point of tears. But once she had calmed down, she warned herself that on no account must she place ready trust in anything – neither must she readily believe propaganda nor must she readily believe facts – even if they were facts. Why? Hadn't her father already made it clear with his dying words two years ago. . .'

She couldn't help beginning to feel disgruntled at her brother's high spirits. She raised her head and looked at him, and found his face glowing with health and happiness that reflected itself in the smile that played about his lips.

'You seem very cheerful today, Xiao Mo.'

'I am.' Shu Mo excitedly flicked the hair from his forehead and clicked his teeth together as if thinking of saying something. But he changed his mind. 'I've got some good news to tell you . . . uh . . . no, there's just one thing . . . I'll tell you when we get home.'

He called it home, but in fact it was no more than a tiny cellar of less than seven square metres. Not long after their father had died, some people had come from the university and, on the pretext that housing was short and that households in difficulty had to be looked after, had driven the brother and sister from their small room into the cellar of an old Russian-style house. Fortunately Shu Bei seldom came home and Shu Mo solved the problem of space by erecting a small platform for storage over the door.

Shu Bei pushed open the door and saw at first glance that the dark little room had been transformed. The walls had been painted pale green and the rough concrete floor had been smoothed and painted with a layer of shiny red paint. The small, narrow window had been polished sparkling clean and a reproduction of Goya's etching *May Day Festival in Madrid* added a touch of liveliness to the scene. Above the head of one bed hung a horizontal scroll of calligraphy written in a free cursive hand: 'Music should make the soul of mankind send forth sparks – Beethoven'. Shu Mo complacently paced around the little room calling loudly, 'Look! Summer and the Songhua River have come into my heart together!'

Shu Bei went over to the small writing-desk under the window and, as her glance took it in, she couldn't help starting in alarm.

Underneath the glass-plate top had been placed a recently made enlargement of a portrait of her mother. It was a striking likeness, capturing her mother in radiant spirits. Those lovely eyes that kept their true feelings secret gazed at them with kindly tenderness. Under the photograph was a yellowing sheet of creased paper on which was written in an elegant yet hasty hand: 'My people, I love you. You must be vigilant!'

'Xiao Mo, you – ' she choked on her words. 'How could you. . .'

Shu Bei had never dreamed that her brother would be so bold as to display under the glass the words that her mother had written just before throwing herself to her death twelve years ago. What if visitors saw it? How ignorant of the ways of the world her brother was! This was the second stupid thing that Shu Mo had done that Shu Bei had seen with her own eyes in the last few days. In the past year he had changed enormously and seemed to be getting bolder and bolder. Shu Bei couldn't help shivering. Mother had studied in the Soviet Union as a solo soprano and had enjoyed a high reputation in China and abroad. But, as soon as the political campaigns began in 1966, she had been seized on the charge of 'having illicit relations with foreign countries' and being a suspected 'spy'. She had immediately been put into solitary confinement and shortly afterwards, at a mass meeting, had been proclaimed a 'spy of the Soviet revisionists'. Shu Bei had been forced to stand in the front row of spectators and, when she saw her mother, her face swollen from torture, fresh scars on her face and hands, and a pair of high-heeled shoes worn during performances hung around her neck as she knelt barefoot on the stage, she was so distressed that she let out a wail of anguish. The people on the stage began to roar like malignant devils and a vicious blow sent her reeling. Through a blur of tears, she saw her mother, her eyes blazing with fury, leap towards the microphone. But she was quickly dragged down. She did not have the right to speak. It was at that meeting that they had announced that tomorrow her mother would be paraded through the streets of the city with a placard around her neck, making special visits to the units of her two children and her husband to be denounced. She must beat the gong herself and publicly describe all her crimes. An exhibition of photographs taken during her performances would be put on display at the main gates of the opera house.

Shu Bei shook like a withered leaf in the autumn wind. A kind-hearted woman took her home, muttering furiously, 'It's utterly inhuman! Ah, tomorrow!'

'Tomorrow. . .' Shu Bei didn't dare to think of it. 'To-morrow. . .' If those things really happened tomorrow, would her mother still be her mother?

Late that night Shu Bei woke with a start from a nightmare, her body bathed in cold sweat, her heart pounding wildly. She was filled with a premonition of some disaster and, leaping out of bed, stood for a long while with her ear pressed to the door. But apart from the rustling of the wind in the trees outside the window she could hear nothing . . . she cried herself to sleep only to be tortured by one terrifying dream after another. She dreamt of her mother. Could this really be their last sight of each other. Early next morning the sound of violent hammering on the door woke brother and sister with a start. They were ordered to attend the mass denunciation meeting for the Soviet spy x x who had committed suicide to escape punishment. 'Tomorrow' . . . it was tomorrow, but in the end their mother had refused this 'tomorrow'. At midnight she had torn away the paper strips that sealed the window and jumped from the top floor . . . a long time afterwards, an old odd-job man had brought them the crumpled slip of paper on which she had written her last words.

When Li Xin had visited them that time, Shu Mo had taken out the paper with his mother's words and shown it to him (Shu Bei had been too late to stop him). After reading it, Li Xin muttered to himself for a long while, then finally made a comment that Shu Bei would never forget: 'Her death was a protest against the destruction of art and the humiliation of human dignity. She died precisely because she loved life and loved her country too deeply. If she was not allowed to love, she preferred to die.' His words were a sudden revelation to Shu Bei, and she began to feel a new respect for her mother, yet she still felt that her words were too abstract and could not match her father's in their penetrating understanding of reality.

'My people, I love you. You must be vigilant! – the immortal saying of the Czechoslavak revolutionary writer Fučik.' Shu Mo read it aloud and said eagerly, 'Sister, recently I've come to feel more and more strongly that Mama's choice of her last words was really profound!'

'Don't talk to me about love!' Shu Bei suddenly became vexed and coldly cut him short. 'What's the good news you are going to tell me, huh? What is it? Come on, tell me!'

The sparks of enthusiasm shining in Shu Mo's eyes died, his mouth twitched at her harsh attitude and he sat down hugging his shoulders, not saying a word. Finally he shyly blurted out: 'If I tell you, you won't be angry?'

Shu Bei's heart sank. With an effort she replied, 'If I was going to be angry I would have died of anger long ago.' She suddenly thought of something and inquired eagerly, 'Has the opera troupe decided to rehabilitate Mama? I was going to go tomorrow to ask.'

'No,' Shu Mo shook his head, 'I asked about it ages ago. They said they've reported the case to higher levels, but it hasn't been approved yet.'

Shu Bei smiled bitterly. 'I'm afraid it will never be approved. . .'

'No, it's different now, I'm sure it'll be approved very soon,' Shu Mo said confidently.

Shu Bei didn't feel inclined to argue with her brother – in her opinion he was really too childish – so she gave him an inquiring look to urge him to return to the subject.

Shu Mo stood on tiptoe and took the old violin case down from the home-made bookcase. Obviously his news had something to do with his violin. He gave a nervous cough as if it required great resolution to get the words out, and after vigorously coughing a second time, was about to speak when someone knocked at the door.

As if receiving a pardon for some heinous crime, Shu Mo leapt to the door, opened it just a crack and quickly slipped out. The murmur of low voices could be heard in the corridor. After a long time he came back in and winked slyly at Shu Bei, saying apologetically, 'I have to go out, we'll talk more when I get back.' And he was gone in a flash.

5

The strange thing was that Shu Mo had only just gone when there was another knock at the door. Shu Bei was lying on the bed tortuously pondering all that her brother had told her, and had already decided to have a serious talk with him when he returned. In the midst of her troubled thoughts, a sudden 'Is Shu Bei at home?' in a warm baritone made her heart leap wildly. Before she had time to get up, the visitor, not standing on ceremony, had pushed open the door and walked lightly into the room.

It was he who had appeared so often in her dreams – tall with thick spectacles behind which flashed the brilliance of penetrating thought. He stood a little constrainedly before her, a book tucked under his arm, gazing at her with a slight smile.

'Are you feeling better?' He seemed to think up this question only with great difficulty.

'Um,' she nodded her head and answered almost inaudibly.

For some reason this was followed by a long silence. The two of them both lowered their heads and sat without exchanging a word.

Shu Bei surreptitiously peeped at him out of the corner of her eye: He was sitting a few paces from her, close enough to her, yet so far away? At a time like this if she had vacillated a little, if she had spoken just a single word, they would have compliantly become the captives of emotion. But she was incapable of it. She was no longer a child. If she could have, she would have liked to hang the word 'love' on a steel anchor and sink it forever in the depths of the Songhua River. Why should a person living in this world want to love? Couldn't she think of a hundred examples to prove that nobody who loved life ever came to a good end, while on the contrary those scoundrels, who had never loved anyone or only loved themselves, rose rapidly in the world? Despite the fact that the Gang of Four had been toppled, weren't all those people still around? Although today one could perform Sarasate's dances in the main street and play a guitar in one's swimsuit by the Songhua River, what about tomorrow? Who could tell what it would be like then? Her father's dying words were correct: when you link your destiny to that of another person, what you must first consider is not whether you love him or not, but whether or not you will be able to live in this world in safety. The young man sitting a few feet away from her was a wonderful person, but why couldn't he have been a worker or a technician instead of a lover of philosophy, a recently rehabilitated 'active counter-revolutionary'? All day long his head was filled with bold, unorthodox ideas. In the face of harsh reality, this kind of person was most likely to fall. Hadn't her own and her family's misfortunes over the last ten years taught her long since: 'Keep away from politics'! Her respect for her father's dying words did not stem from the feudal concept that 'Father's will must not be violated', but from the conviction that the instructions her father gave her on his deathbed could protect her shattered heart from being wounded again.

But contrary to reason, her brother stubbornly loved something he ought not to love; and she had fallen in love with someone who was the last person she should have loved. Ah, life, why do you have to throw such knotty problems before someone who has no strength to solve them?

'Beini,' Li Xin finally plucked up enough courage to break the silence, 'did you get my letter?'

The painful moment had to come sooner or later, so it might as well be sooner. She lowered her eyes to avoid his fervent gaze and said as calmly as possible, 'Yes . . . uh, but it's already too late. . .'

'Too late?' He was puzzled. 'Why?'

'Because, because . . . because I . . . already have a boy . . . boyfriend.'

'No! That's impossible!' He cried out involuntarily.

'It's true,' she said coldly.

He leant dejectedly against the back of the chair, and for a long time didn't say a word.

Shu Bei felt terrible and turned her head away, afraid that those flashing spectacles would penetrate her innermost being.

He suddenly stood up and walked over to her, his expression calm yet determined, but his face a little pale. His flashing eyes gazed at her questioningly yet they were full of warmth.

'I only ask that you answer one question.' He spoke as if it required all his energy to speak. 'Did you ever love me?'

He received no reply.

From her long silence, he guessed that she was unwilling to give the reply that would make his situation unbearably awkward. He began to tremble and slowly made his way towards the door. At the doorway he turned and stretched out his hand to shake hers in farewell. She did not respond, but sat biting her lips hard, her face ashen. He gazed at her intently, then sighed lightly, and resolutely turned his back. He was about to pull open the door when Shu Bei suddenly leapt up sobbing and threw her arms around his shoulders.

'I love you,' she cried. 'I love you. No one has ever made me love so deeply! I have always longed for . . . I'll never love anyone but you. . .'

But this sudden passionate cry from the heart did not bring Li Xin any sense of elation. He stood for a moment in silence, then said calmly, 'To tell the truth, I sensed it long ago. It was just that you weren't willing and wouldn't dare to admit it.'

'But, I. . .' Shu Bei raised her tear-stained face, not knowing how to frame her words. No matter how she put it, it would not be appropriate. She hesitated, and for several seconds gazed dully into Li Xin's face.

'I beg you to choose between me and your philosophy and politics. If you love me then don't have anything more to do with social science, it's a pit of hell, a snare, I know . . . I love you, but I don't love your philosophy. Don't you understand my circumstances, my feelings?'

Her burning cheek pressed against Li Xin's chest and her tears rolled down wetting the front of his shirt.

'You really mean I must choose one or the other?' he asked in a low voice, brushing the wet hair from her face.

'Yes.'

'Then my reply will disappoint you, Beini,' he said calmly. 'I can't abandon the career I love because I love you. I can't. I love you and I love my career too – there's no inconsistency in that. I thought that we had a lot of experiences in common, that our hearts beat in harmony, but I never imagined. . .'

The colour drained from Shu Bei's face. She quickly released him and walked over to the other side of the room.

For a long time she stood silently before the desk lost in thought while the golden rays of the setting sun played over her hair. Then, with her back to Li Xin, she grasped the window frame and suddenly demanded resolutely, 'Then perhaps you can tell me, in another twenty or thirty years time, will the tragedy of my father's generation be re-enacted? Tell me. . .'

Li Xin shook his head earnestly. 'I have no way of knowing. I'm not a fortune-teller and I don't intend to open an insurance company, but I think you understand that mankind only traverses the path to freedom at an enormous cost. Countless materialists have already sacrificed themselves to light the lamp of science. You

know that Bruno was sentenced to be burned at the stake for opposing religion. If our generation is not prepared to sacrifice itself for science, then how can we even talk about working towards the "four modernizations"?'

Ten years earlier, Shu Bei would have been deeply stirred by Li Xin's lofty ideals and would have unhesitatingly taken his hand and walked bravely into the future. But now she had no courage, no courage to face squarely that great and terrifying word 'self-sacrifice'. Her eyes widened in blank despair.

'OK. Let's not talk about it now.' Li Xin looked at his watch and discovered that he was still holding the book in his hand. His black brows twitched rapidly as if concealing deep suffering. 'In the past I always hoped that the one I loved would love life and esteem the truth as I do. I still cherish that hope and always will do . . . Oh, I brought this book for you, so I may as well give it to you.' He lightly placed the book on the table and pulled the door open. The sound of his heavy footsteps faded into the distance.

Shu Bei stood in a daze staring expressionlessly at a perspiration stain he had left on the brand-new book cover. It was a reprint of *Spartacus*. She stared at it for a long time, then suddenly clasped the book to her breast and threw herself down on the bed.

6

Some time later, Shu Bei raised her head and saw that it was already dark. She turned on the light, and only then discovered that Shu Mo had been sitting there in the dark, his head in his hands. She couldn't help being startled by the anger in his face.

'What's the matter? What are you thinking about?' Shu Bei asked flurriedly.

'I'm considering whether I want to go on living or not.' The corners of Shu Mo's mouth carried an obvious sneer. 'I'm obviously in love with somebody, but I "fear wolves ahead and tigers behind". I have endless misgivings and am terrified of violating some "divine law". I have no interest in life, so. . .'

'Xiao Mo!' Shu Bei glared at him sorrowfully, 'Don't be so acrimonious. . .' Now she understood that Li Xin's arrival and Shu Mo's departure had been carefully engineered.

The lock of black hair on Shu Mo's forehead trembled, revealing both his agitation and the fact that he had no intention of showing

his usual reverence for his sister. He was outraged at the cold treatment that Li Xin had suffered in the past week and at the refusal his sister had just given, and felt even he himself had been humiliated. All the words he had held back for so long, now exploded forth:

'When I read *Liang Shanbo and Zhu Yingtai* and *Records of the Western Chamber*, I thought that they were only stories of the feudal society, but today I have discovered that you don't even have the courage of Zhu Yingtai or Cui Yingying. When the Gang of Four were toppled, you were more elated than anyone, yet in the last year you have fallen far behind the times. You don't dare to love, don't dare to laugh, don't dare to speak, don't dare to get angry. In order to refuse Li Xin, you went and said you already have a boyfried on the commune. You're talking rubbish!'

Shu Bei covered her face with her hands and mumbled. 'Xiao Mo, it's true . . . I've already done as Papa instructed and asked comrades to find me the most ordinary of young men, a fitter . . . though it hasn't been finally fixed yet, I think maybe I'll go along with it and that'll be the end of the matter. . .'

Astonishment and fury rendered Shu Mo speechless for a long time.

'Do you . . . do you love that fitter?'

'No – I don't know. . .' She lowered her eyes to avoid his threatening gaze.

Shu Mo silently pulled a tiny slip of paper out of his pocket and said gravely, 'OK. Now I should tell you my good news. To me it really is a piece of glad tidings – I took the exams for the conservatory of music and I've been accepted.'

Shu Bei started as if she had been stung, and her face flushed with anger. She lowered her head and looked at the slip of paper. As the large, bold type of the 'notification of university admittance' swam before her eyes, she realized what it was that her brother had been hiding from her all year. Her lips moved but uttered no sound. She seemed to want to remind him of the time in 1973 when he had taken examinations to join the philharmonic orchestra but had been rejected because he did not have the political qualifications; or remind him how their father had submitted countless reports before being able to get him transferred back from the farm on the grounds of 'special consideration', but she didn't say anything.

———

'Why, why not be a worker. . .' She finally spoke with a great effort.

Shu Mo stroked the letter of notification and replied quickly, 'I'm not unwilling to be a worker, but I've loved music since I was small, and many of my teachers said that I could achieve much as a musician. Why should I force myself not to love it? Perhaps some people think that being a technician provides a secure job, but music is my life, is more important to me than life. I love it so much that if I had to leave it for a single day I couldn't go on living. . .'

Hot tears poured from his large, bright eyes. Shu Bei had not seen her brother so grief-stricken for a long time, and those cascading tears seemed to grind across her heart like a heavy roller. She felt her strength rapidly deserting her.

'Promise me you won't go! You'll understand one day!' she suddenly demanded in a commanding tone.

'No. I don't understand why you're acting like this. Why?'

Shu Bei's eyes glittered as coldly as a snow drift in a shaded mountain gorge. 'Why? Because I believe in nothing!'

'You may not believe in anything, but I do! I believe the People will never allow the tragedies of these ten years to be re-enacted. History has already reached a major turning-point!' Shu Mo shouted excitedly. 'A new era. . .'

'Don't go on, it's no use.' Gasping for breath, Shu Bei cut him short. 'Can you possibly be unaware that by entering the conservatory of music you are treading the path that Papa and Mama followed? At every turn is a precipice so deep that you can't even see the bottom. I'm willing to make a concession and agree to your playing your violin in your spare time, but I beg you to promise me not to make it your career. Promise me!' Shu Bei shook her brother's shoulders, almost entreating him.

'No!' Shu Mo angrily pushed away her hands.

This action, bordering on roughness, seemed to stab at Shu Bei's heart, and a terrifying gloom veiled her eyes.

'Do you promise?' she asked.

Shu Mo resolutely shook his head.

She grabbed the letter of notification from the table.

'What are you doing?' Shu Mo shouted.

Shu Bei laughed coldly and clenched the letter tightly in her fist. But her hand was shaking.

Suddenly realizing that his sister might tear the letter to shreds, Shu Mo became so anxious that beads of sweat began to form on his forehead. He gazed at Shu Bei's anguished face with troubled eyes, and in his distress, his hands clenched tightly into fists.

'You, you haven't . . . no one has the right, no one has the right to prevent me from loving!' he finally shouted out and violently crashed his fist down on the glass-topped desk. The glass shattered and crimson blood trickled on to the fading, black characters beneath.

That shout was like an arrow that pierces the wild goose's wing. Shu Bei shuddered and her arm dropped limply, the letter of notification fluttering lightly to the floor.

'Right?' she raised her eyebrows coldly. 'You're talking about rights? It's true, I have no right. . .' Tears filled her eyes, but did not fall. It seemed as if they were flowing into her heart. 'But have you ever thought about whether we have the right to love or not? Do we? Think about the past twelve years. Didn't we long ago lose any rights we ever had? From as far back as I can remember I have never thought of demanding any rights from society. Mama didn't even have the right to love the people and Papa had even less right to love his career. And as for me, wasn't the right to find work back here in our home town and the right to have a love affair wrested from me long ago? And you still talk of rights. . . !' Bitter tears finally gushed from her despairing eyes and splashed on to the floor. 'I, I only have the right to be a good nurse. It's enough. I long since stopped thinking about anything. I want nothing. . .' She buried her face in her arms and sobbed broken-heartedly, her sobs so laden with grief it seemed she wanted to wash away all the sorrows of the last years with her tears.

Never before had Shu Mo known that so deep a wound lay buried in his sister's heart. When his mother had died he was still very young, and not long after the death of his father he had welcomed back the light into his life. After one has woken, the memory of a nightmare fades quickly, and hopes and ideals are always sacred to the young. During the hard times, brother and sister had depended on one another for survival and Shu Bei had always concealed her grief in order to bring her brother a pitiful ray of happiness. Shu Mo loved his sister, and if later when he found himself at the crossroads of seeking the truth in life he had not met

Li Xin – that bold warrior who dared to think and dared to act – he would perhaps have revered his sister's words as infallible. But Li Xin very quickly came to occupy his sister's position in his ideology. For the first time Li Xin pointed the truth out to him and helped him to find sweet springs in the midst of his parched wilderness, to find the right path without meandering through as many tortuous by-roads as other young people of his age. He learned to think deeply and search out the origins of his own family's misfortunes. He matured quickly and entered the ranks of the 'heretics'. After the fall of the Gang of Four, he became even more full of confidence in the future and would not even listen to anyone who raised any doubts. He was like a ball of fire and, like fire fearing water, kept his distance from his ice-cold sister, grumbled at her and secretly reproved her. Behind her back he began to do all the things he wanted to do, and even felt that by doing so he was expressing his brotherly affection to the fullest. But only now did he realize that he had been utterly mistaken. His heart ached in spasms as if someone was squeezing it tightly, and he felt that he had never before had such pity for Shu Bei.

'Sister,' he said in his gentlest tones, wringing out a hot towel and handing it to her, 'think about it, why can't I love the career that I love? Why can't you love the man that you love? As socialist citizens, each of us has those rights – just as long as that man is one of the people and that career is in the interests of the people. If you say that many good-hearted people had their right to love their country and their people stripped from them by the Gang of Four in those dark years, then haven't millions of the masses of the people already seized those rights back again? Yet you actually want to abandon those rights yourself. . .'

'It's true, I'd rather abandon. . .' she spoke almost inaudibly.

'Darling Sister, you've been wounded too deeply. The heat of summer is approaching, but it's as if you're still wearing a padded jacket and headscarf. Open your eyes and take a good look – now even the glaciers have begun to melt. . .'

Shu Mo, bubbling over with enthusiasm, threw open the curtains and the strong fragrance of flowers wafted through the window on the evening breeze.

'Li Xin wanted me to tell you that though you prefer to hold yourself aloof from the world to protect yourself for the rest of your

life and avoid the fate of our parents. In reality that's just not possible. The only way out is to put up a fight. Only when the people in their millions have mastered the weapons of science and democracy will their right to love never again be wrested from them!'

Raising her head, Shu Bei gazed at her brother through a blur of tears and felt that he had become a stranger to her. When had he changed into a philosopher?

Shu Mo stood up and with a grim expression walked over to her bed and pulled out the white envelope from the satchel she always carried with her. He calmly struck a match.

'What are you going to do?' She felt the terror rising within her.

'This was originally an accusation that Papa left behind, but you have made it into an excuse for your own weakness and cowardice.' Shu Mo, head high, spoke with assurance. 'I can't let it go with us into the twenty-first century. I believe that if Papa were alive today he would surely take it back and alter it. I'm certain he would seize his due rights back from those fascist butchers! I'm definitely going to music school, I want to dedicate my whole life to music. And if one day I fall in love with a girl, no matter who she is, just as long as she's worthy of my love, then I will love her courageously, love her, love her to the end!'

Flames licked hungrily at the tiny envelope, and in a moment it was reduced to ashes.

Shu Bei had no idea why she hadn't stopped him. In the light of the flames she had seen those beautiful, thoughtful eyes in her mother's portrait flashing brilliantly; and the line of characters on her last letter seemed themselves to be about to burst into flames.

7

In this cold northern city, even though summer did not always make its approach felt, it did, after all, arrive. Only on summer mornings before people had awakened did the sun stain the broad waters of the Songhua River into a sparkling ribbon of colour.

A girl of twenty-seven or twenty-eight slowly climbed on to the deck of the passenger steamer leaving for a county town on the lower reaches of the river. The boat would not leave for a while and she distractedly gazed at the river embankment as if waiting for something. She was leaving secretly without saying goodbye because she felt there was nothing she could say. She needed time to think, to ponder things over from beginning to end.

On the embankment she could see people cycling to work; old folk in the shade of the willows practising shadow boxing and wielding swords; young people tucked away in pavilions reciting vocabulary in foreign languages; and young mothers pushing light prams, playing with their plump babies as they strolled along. Beneath the commemorative monument a huge work of art was on display surrounded by a crowd of appreciative viewers. Everyone looked relaxed and happy, their faces radiant.

'Ah – ' Shu Bei heaved a long sigh and longed to shout out to them, 'Please tell me, are you all loving the things and people that you love?'

The only answer she received was the drawn-out whistle of the boat's siren as it drew away from its moorings.

Two figures appeared, cycling furiously towards the dock. They leapt off their bikes and rushed on to the embankment waving at the steamer and shouting in unison, 'Shu Bei – '

Shu Bei's eyes grew moist with tears and she couldn't stop herself from pulling out her handkerchief and waving it at them.

They saw her. The tall, bespectacled young man shaped his hands into a funnel and shouted to her, 'I'll come to see you in the summer holidays. . .'

The sound of that gentle, kindly baritone rippled across the surface of the river and finally merged with its surging waters.

She listened attentively to the roar of the waves and felt that each surging billow was knocking on the door of her heart and bringing her a delicious warmth such as she had never felt before.

It suddenly occurred to her that she was always afraid that the bright, beautiful summer would pass and the harsh winter return, but even if the great river did freeze over, wasn't the surging torrent still rushing onwards beneath the thick layer of ice? This was a tide that could not be held back, it was a right that no one could take away.

'My people, I love you. . .' She unwittingly spoke the words aloud. Tears welled from her eyes and she quickly wiped them away.

From some unknown place, the emotion-charged strains of a violin floated to her ears. At first she thought she must be imagining it, but she wasn't. The violin was clearly playing a tune very familiar to her: 'Little track so narrow, o'er the wide plains twists. . .' She stood blankly for a moment, then raised her head in search of those notes that seemed to come to her like a ray of brilliant sunshine. But all she could see was the boundless river racing joyfully into the vast distance. She continued to seek out the violinist and, as she searched, her heart began to sing along lightly with his melody.

Translated by R. A. Roberts

THE POETIC SOUL
OF YOUYAN*

DING NING

Great ocean ah! You are the most beautiful poetry.
Hidden deep in your broad bosom is a pure poetic soul.
Poetic soul! Won't you come back?

A DOZEN OR more years ago, on the shores of the Bohai Sea in lovely Beidaihe, was a tiny sanatorium for members of the literary world. Each year with the coming of summer, the atmosphere would begin to liven up. A steady stream of writers, literary workers and artists would arrive in their twos and threes, gathering there to let the azure sea cleanse their bodies of dust and the cool breeze stroke the sweat from their foreheads. The beautiful scenery on those perfect days presented an opportunity too good to be missed: the industrious writers spread open their manuscripts and continued to absorb themselves in their writing.

In early July 1961, I paid my first visit to this famous summer resort and on the day of my arrival went to view the sea. That great ocean stretched vast and boundless before me, yet I felt its

* Youyan is an alternative name for the area of Hebei Province in which Beidaihe is located. The name is taken from that of two ancient towns in the region, Youzhou and Yanzhou.

profundity was quite unfathomable. On my return, I found the sanatorium dining room reverberating with a heated debate as several comrades probed the secrets of the sea: sometimes it was gentle, sometimes brutal. Was it kindly or vicious? How should one ultimately assess its nature?

'Provided you are willing to understand it, you will find it embodies the courage and wisdom of the people.'

Who was this man with such unique views? It was none other than Comrade Yang Shuo. He was always quiet and refined, and not adept at debate, but he had been born and raised on the sea-shore, he loved and understood the sea, so he argued with authority.

Yang Shuo was a comrade highly respected by all. He was always neatly dressed in spotless clothing and was well-mannered and soft-spoken, yet he gave one the feeling that he was a solitary man, that there was something mysterious buried in the depths of his heart. I worked in the same unit as he, yet I knew little about him.

When his simple luggage – a battered old travelling bag – was first carried into a room in a little red-brick building, he modestly declined to mount the stairs for quite some time. The building contained the best accommodation in the sanatorium, and Yang Shuo, accustomed to years of rough outdoor living on the battlefield, was naturally unwilling to accept special privileges.

'You can watch the sea from upstairs.'

'You can enjoy a grander sight

By climbing to a greater height.'*

Warmly urged on by his comrades, Yang Shuo finally climbed to the second storey.

Early next morning the canteen was once more a scene of cheer and humour. Yang Shuo in his poetic language was describing his impressions of his first night's sleep in the building: the wild waves, roaring like ten thousand horsemen riding into battle, had seemed to take him back to the battlefield where for days on end the roar of gunfire never ceased. He had become intoxicated with the excitement of slaying the enemy. Deep in the night when everything was still, the wind and waves had played a majestic symphony, a sweet-sounding lullaby that had carried him into a wonderful fairy-land. . . His conclusion: the sea is the most beautiful poetry.

* Lines from 'On the Stork Tower' by Wang Zhihuan (688–742) a famous poet of the Tang Dynasty.

That evening the moon shone brilliantly, and comrades strolled together on the moonlit sands admiring the night seascape. The sea and sky merged in the hazy distance, silvery wavelets sparkled. The great sea was more tranquil, more mysterious than ever. Spindrift lightly stroked the shore as the waves rolled in, one after another, as if singing, as if in accusation. Without the need for prior agreement, comrades began to recite, 'There was a fresh, gentle breeze, but the water was unruffled. . . . We chanted the poem on the bright moon, singing the stanza about the fair maid'.* Someone suggested to an artist that he should paint a night seascape, but before he could answer, Yang Shuo spoke. 'A night seascape is not hard to paint, what is difficult is to express the profound soul of the sea.' Another comrade proposed that each of us should recite a poem – it could be classical or modern, but every poem must contain the word 'moon'. When it came to Yang Shuo's turn, he took up an elegant stance and in a clear, resonant voice recited Su Dongpo's 'Bright Moon': 'Bright moon, when was your birth? Wine cup in hand, I ask the deep blue sky; not knowing what year it is tonight, in those celestial palaces on high.' As he reached the lines 'My one wish for you, then, is long life, and a share in this loveliness far, far away!', his voice suddenly grew hoarse and his expression became vague and distant. I couldn't help wondering: was he thinking of a comrade-in-arms, or a loved one? Perhaps in some far-away place was one who owned his heart.

The writers began to discuss poetry. They all declared that this poem by Su Shi was profound in conception and artistically outstanding. Heaven and earth, fantasy and reality were fused into one. It was the perfect example of the combination of realism and romanticism in classical poetry.

Yang Shuo had a special love of Su Dongpo's poetry. Once he came back from a sightseeing tour in exuberant spirits, and rapidly jotted down another of Su Shi's poems. The last verse ran: 'Who says that youth never returns? Look, river water can still turn and flow westwards. Don't grieve over your white hair, brace yourself!

---

* Lines taken from 'First Visit to the Red Cliff' by Su Shi. Su Shi (1037–1101), also known as Su Dongpo, was the leading poet and prose writer of the Northern Song period as well as a celebrated calligrapher and painter. He was a distinguished statesman and held many official posts, but was also banished several times during his life.

Never be pessimistic.' He eulogized the active optimism expressed in these lines of the great poet: 'Since the ancients could harbour such sentiments, how can we communists fail to be revolutionary optimists?'

He not only loved poetry, but also had his own unique views on it. In one essay he wrote that, in writing fiction and prose, he frequently sought a poetic conception: 'I have always loved poetry, particularly those classical poems that have stood the test of the centuries. Almost every one of those poems has its own fresh artistic conception, ideology and emotions, affording much food for thought.' As to the meaning of 'poetic quality', he believed: 'Almond blossoms and spring rain can certainly constitute poetry, but the heroic spirit embodied in war-horses and the glint of weapons possesses more poetic power to rouse men's hearts. In the midst of struggle, labour, life, there are many things that move one, excite one, make one joyful or sorrowful, make one think deeply. If this is not poetry, then what is it?'

Yang Shuo was constantly searching for poetry. He lived every moment within the artistic conception of poetry. He had his own particular interests, liked to ponder deeply, and was fond of chatting with friends. He loved to seek the significance of the topic under discussion and discover its underlying philosophy. His room was always very quiet, with just the low sound of recitation floating out on an occasional gust of light wind: that was Yang Shuo learning foreign languages and reciting poetry.

Early each morning he would go out alone, leaving a solitary trail of footprints in the sand. The wooden hills would reverberate with his footsteps as he paced up and down, and when he returned, his shirt would be speckled with the wet stains of dew drops.

Once I asked him, 'Don't you feel lonely strolling alone?'

He replied, 'No, I talk with the sea.'

'What pleasure do you find in the depths of the forest?'

' "Wild flowers burgeoning and blooming with a secret fragrance, the stately trees put on their mantle of leaves and give a goodly shade," ' he quoted in response from Ouyang Xiu's 'The Roadside Hut of the Old Drunkard'.

One night a heavy storm raged through the sanatorium orchard. The small apple trees and the slender peaches were blown askew and some lay on the ground like children who had been bullied.

Yang Shuo rose at first light, and with great compassion, took a spade and carefully propped them up one by one, banking new earth around them. The manager of the sanatorium, Old Zhao, was an honest, industrious 'horticulturist' whom Yang Shuo held in the highest esteem. He kept the large orchard pruned and trimmed to perfection, so that pears and peaches bowed the branches with their weight and the fragrance of all kinds of apples scented the air. Yang Shuo often expressed his admiration: 'When Old Zhao is at work, he is not only dextrous, but possesses a kind of beauty. There is a sense of rhythm and a musical quality to his labour. Labour really does create art, and Old Zhao is a genuine artist!'

Old Zhao plucked a juicy red peach from the broken branch of a peach tree and affectionately presented it to Yang Shuo. Yang Shuo placed it on a plate like a treasured gift, and humorously asked Old Zhao: 'Wasn't this stolen from the Queen Mother of the West's Feast of Peaches?'* The honest Old Zhao defended himself stoutly. 'Stolen? It was grown on our own fruit trees and that's the truth.' Old Zhao advised Yang Shuo that it was food and not a plaything, and should be eaten immediately, but Yang Shuo disagreed with him. 'This is a work of art you have created. How could I have the heart to demolish it?' Quite at a loss, the simple Old Zhao shook his head good-naturedly.

Yang Shuo was born on the Jiaodong Peninsula in the 'Penglai Fairyland'† so rich in mythological tradition. He left home as a youth, but often thought longingly of his native region. He always took great delight in talking of home town affairs and would speak and listen with lively interest. He was most interested in the deeds of the army and people in Jiaodong during the years of the war. I would relate my stories to him over and over again, and he would listen in delight with half-closed eyes, never feeling he had heard enough. Sometimes as he was listening he would exclaim in admiration, 'That is stirring poetry.' Once I told him the story of how one of my schoolmates had resisted the Japanese: she was a beautiful girl who was attending a wartime middle school. Once

* This refers to an incident in the classical novel *Journey to the West* in which the Monkey King steals peaches of longevity intended for the Queen Mother of the West's Feast of Peaches.
† Penglai Fairyland: the mythological home of Chinese immortals, believed to be in the Jiaodong region.

when the Japanese were carrying out mopping-up operations, she fastened a hand grenade to her waist and went along to hide under a bed in the home of a villager. As a horde of Japanese broke into the room, she didn't wait to be discovered, but boldly leapt into their midst and exploded the grenade: Japanese and traitors to China died where they stood. . .'

'And what about her?' he asked urgently.

'She was only wounded, but when I went to visit her later in hospital, her beautiful raven hair was completely gone.'

'It's simply a miracle! Perhaps an immortal protected the brave girl. But where is she now?'

'That I don't know.'

Then there was a long silence, and looking at him, I saw his face clouded with pain and desolation. His expression made me recall a popular story that people used to tell about him:

A long time ago, probably while he was still a middle-school student, he came to know a lovely girl from his home town. They gradually grew to love and trust one another. Later when he left his home to work for the revolution, they pledged a troth of eternal love. Through the long years the girl waited for him, and as time flew past, she turned from twenty to thirty without ever seeing a sign of her lover. The enemy occupied her home town, and her sorrow turned to despair. Finally she bade her last farewell to the world. After the war, when he returned to his home town, the soul of the girl had already wandered far away, but he never stopped searching for it.

Was the story true or false? It was likely that no one had ever asked him. What would be the point? If it were true, was there any need to re-open old wounds? And if it were false, then there was even less need to discredit this moving tale. But one thing could be confirmed: he had always remained single. Everyone felt that there was someone who existed in his heart.

Yang Shuo's most treasured possession was a notebook with a tattered cover that he carried with him wherever he went. In it he had recorded a wealth of battle stories gathered from his own experiences during the war and from his interviews of other people. Each time he opened the notebook he would say proudly, 'This is full of poetry!' Apart from its pages of closely written characters, the book also contained some specimens of dried flowers, most of

---

them gathered on the battlefields of North Korea. There was wild winter jasmine, and a pink azalea, all plucked long ago and now dull and colourless. Looking at them, Yang Shuo would sigh and exclaim: 'If only flowers did not wither, leaves did not fall, and all beautiful things could live for ever.' He told me that each of these specimens had a moving tale to it, and specially related to me the story behind that pink azalea. It had been given to him by a heroine of the volunteer army. The woman, named Ning, was a doctor in the volunteer corps. Once, during an enemy bombing raid, she had been wounded and lost consciousness. When she came to she suddenly heard a voice behind her calling, 'Doctor, doctor!' Turning around she found a comrade buried to the chest in earth. Disregarding her own pain, she dug with her fingers until her fingernails bled, but she could not dig the man out. Bombs were still exploding around them, and the buried comrade shouted to her, 'Get out of here fast. Don't worry about me.' But she replied resolutely, 'No, I'm going to dig you out.' Finally the soldier was free, and taking him on her back, she braved the hail of enemy bullets to carry him to safety. But on the way they came upon another wounded comrade lying immobile on the ground. She carried the first man up the mountain, then returned for the second. But once the second soldier had been carried to safety, she became aware that she herself was wounded in four or five places and her clothing was soaked with blood. Her last strength exhausted, she collapsed to the ground. Later, she was saved by somebody else and, after recovery, returned to work on the front line.

'But what about the azalea?'

'The soldier she had dug out later picked it from the pile of earth he had been buried in and gave it to her.'

'And how did you get it?'

'When I interviewed her on the Korean battlefield, she gave the precious flower to me.'

Yang Shuo finished his story and took a photograph from the notebook. I saw a delicate-featured, short-haired woman of no more than twenty in the uniform of the volunteer corps.

'This is Doctor Ning.'

With the greatest respect, I gazed intently at the photograph of the heroine.

'She has a magnificent poetic soul. She was born and raised in a heroic era. Heroic eras produce heroes.' He spoke to himself as if reciting a poem.

Yang Shuo had recorded this story in the 1950s in a piece of prose writing entitled 'Age of Heroes', but it was not until a long time afterwards that I heard that he had not told the whole story, but had deleted its stirring finale. He had interviewed the woman doctor on the battlefield and she had just begun to speak into the microphone when enemy bombers began another attack. Suddenly realizing that they were in the direct line of fire, Yang Shuo moved like lightning: he pushed the woman into a nearby trench, and holding her medical kit in his arms dived for cover. When the enemy planes were gone they found a huge piece of shrapnel lying in the place where they had just been sitting. But when he wrote 'Age of Heroes' Yang Shuo omitted this exciting final episode.

An endless succession of visitors came to the sanatorium, and no matter whose visitors they were, they would bring delight to everyone there. One day a delicate-featured, short-haired young woman came to visit Yang Shuo. It was clear that her arrival brought him enormous pleasure. Who was she? Everyone curiously made their guesses.

They strolled together on the beach, their laughter mingling loud and clear.

'Who is your guest?'

'The most adorable person,' he replied.

In delighted surprise I suddenly recognized her – she was Doctor Ning!

But Yang Shuo indicated that his guest did not wish her name to be known, and merely said that she was a doctor currently working in a hospital at Qinhuangdao. That afternoon a man in army uniform arrived who turned out to be the woman's husband. The three of them went for an intimate stroll at the water's edge, and recited together a poem of soldiers of the volunteer corps:

We will never forget
The names of our fallen comrades.
We will eternally cherish
Friendships pledged on the battlefield.

Silhouetted against the brilliant, colourful evening clouds, they seemed to have entered a world of living artistry.

Only afterwards did I learn that when Doctor Ning left, Yang Shuo returned the pink azalaea to her as the most precious gift he could offer.

Happy times passed swiftly and, before we knew it, several months had passed. One morning a cold breeze and the pattering of heavy rain heralded the beginning of autumn. Without eating any breakfast, I hurried out through the rain to look at the sea. Clouds and mist filled the vast seascape, tempestuous waves crashed on to the silent beach. Making my way through the curtain of rain, I discovered a man standing a little way in front of me, his feet in the sea spray, his clothing soaked. It was Yang Shuo.

'Are you listening to the rain on the water?' I asked.

'No, I'm looking for the footprints of that great man. He probably stood just here, reciting his brilliant poetry.'

Together we began to recite, 'Great rains on Youyan, white waves foam sky-high. . .'* Just then we suddenly caught sight of a figure not far away, momentarily rising high on the crest of a wave and then disappearing once more into the depths. Yang Shuo uttered a cry, ran forward several paces and plunged into the sea. But he was taken unawares by the towering crest of another wave and hurled down into the churning whirlpool beneath. At this moment of crisis he was lightly pulled from the deep water by the very person we had seen battling the waves a moment before. Unexpectedly he turned out to be a youth! His lips trembled with the cold as he stood before us with a mischievous look in his eyes.

'What are you fooling around with your life in this kind of weather for?' Yang Shuo admonished him in tones that betrayed his anger.

'Who are your parents?' I asked.

The youth made no reply. Scornfully sizing up the two 'drenched chickens' standing on the shore, he suddenly burst into laughter, then plunged back into the waves and disappeared.

After a long silence Yang Shuo sighed as if enlightenment had suddenly dawned upon him: 'I was being a timid coward!'

Then we continued our recitation: 'Soughing winds of autumn are here once more, changing the world.'

By this time I already knew that Yang Shuo was to return to Beijing early to attend to some important external affairs.

* Lines from 'Beidaihe', a poem by Mao Zedong.

90

I said regretfully, 'You're leaving, and your poetic soul will leave with you.'

'No,' he replied, 'I want to leave it to the sea, I want the sea to wash it clean.'

Seven years, eight years passed. Who could have imagined that in 1968 this gifted writer would be persecuted by Lin Biao and the Gang of Four? That flaming poetic heart ceased to beat. Just as he wrote in one of his poems:

> I possess a poetic heart that rages like a fire,
> I give up my life, never regretting that I will mingle with the dust.

Another ten years have passed, but I believe that his pure poetic soul is still bounding, full of life, in the depths of the ocean.

Translated by R. A. Roberts

HOW DID I MISS YOU?

ZHANG XINXIN

SATURDAY EVENING HAD come round once again. As usual the trolley-bus raced past the stops along the familiar, bustling street.

As usual she was busy issuing and checking tickets, and as usual she squeezed back and forth through the tightly packed passengers. If it hadn't been for the constant sound of that flat, monotonous tone all the conductresses used to call the names of the stops, which disguised her own pleasant, mellow voice, and for the shapeless blue cotton padded jacket with an artificial fur collar that she was wearing, it could have been hard to pick her out in that sea of blue and grey. She stood at the door, jumping on and off as the bus started and stopped, wearing a pair of high, tight-fitting pigskin boots coated in mud. Brusquely she hustled the passengers on and off, or even simply gave them a shove. When she accidentally knocked against the group of youths, they immediately broke into their usual shouts.

'Hey you! Stupid idiot!'

'Ooh! you're pressing right in the small of my back, missus!'

Like puppy dogs whose tails have been trodden on, some of the lads were loath to pass up the opportunity of expressing their delicate sensibilities. Only as the words left their lips would it dawn upon them – it's her! She never lets you get away with anything! Once provoked she can let fly with some really cutting remarks which are even harder to counter than the stream of curses some girls come out with!

But this time she walked off down the bus as if she hadn't heard! '??!!' There was no understanding her.

In that brief lull in the hustle and bustle no one could have noticed her silently staring out of the bus window – everything was much the same as usual, except for an extra layer of snow, falling in a fine flurry and quietly melting. But to her eyes everything had a sameness about it.

'Don't hang about! Put them here!' Someone she knew had got on the bus. It was Huang Yun, a worker, telling her husband to toss the big frozen fish he was carrying on to the conductor's platform.

Instantly the fresh, briny smell of fish wafted all over the bus.

'Oh! You're still here?!. . . Isn't it you who's written a play? I saw the playbill on a wall next to the Xidan Vegetable Market. Lots of the young people at our factory saw it too, and they've been asking me all about you – what was your name, and so on. Hey, how did that private little matter of yours turn out in the end? When you have so many to choose from it's sometimes hard to pick a good one! Li Ke is so straightforward and simple, don't you think? He'll do just fine! Is he at Beijing University? Or was it the Normal University? A four-year course? That's too long! . . . We don't have a free evening tomorrow either, we've got people coming round for a meal! The extension to our apartment is finished – some friends in the maintenance corps came round and did it for us – I'm hopeless at getting these sorts of things done, I leave it all to him . . . Oh!' Huang Yun abruptly stopped in mid-flow as if she'd had a shock.

Recollecting herself, the conductress stared in surprise at Huang Yun.

'Have you lost something? You look so blank and far-away. What's come over you?'

'I was just wondering if we'd reached the next stop.' She gave a faint smile, but inwardly couldn't help hoping, 'Oh do shut up for a minute, please! I beg you!'

Her gaze flickered between the passengers in the bus and the activity outside, and her hands still kept busy at intervals while at her ear Huang Yun's crisp, quick voice rattled on and on without stopping. However her mind was off on another track, unknown to others, doggedly searching for something. . .

Where are you now? Even if I tell you my true thoughts it's too late!

I arrange predestined encounters for lovers in the world of my imagination, but in real life I find it so hard to find the right one for myself. I know that this may offend a lot of men, wound the feelings of some or attract masculine scorn, but it's an irrepressible sigh which wells up from the bottom of my heart: there really are too few men worthy of being loved!

People say that among today's youth there is an imbalance in the numbers of men and women, but the disappointment I frequently feel is of another kind.

I don't have any admiration for those supermen who manage to squeeze on to the most crowded buses; they are the boys who assume a meditative air when you call on them to give up their seats for others. Nor do I pay any attention to the flashy youths strolling in the streets, the stickers on their teardrop sunglasses proclaiming their up-to-date trendiness, while their faces contain not a trace of inner breeding. We belong to the same generation but I feel we're poles apart. Of course, they wouldn't fall for me either!

As for solid, capable men, the sort like Huang Yun's husband, we can exchange polite nods of greeting, but neither of us thinks anything more than that necessary.

So it's doubly puzzling to me why I have chosen Li Ke, the perfect man. We were at school together right from when we were little, and our fathers both taught at the same middle school for years. Our personal histories in our respective dossiers are alike as two peas in a pod. But we are quite different in temperament. Whenever I get excited about something talking to him, often making no attempt to conceal my laughter, he pulls a long face and sighs, 'You haven't changed a bit! You'll never solve the problems of the party with that attitude.' From his expression it seems as if something terrible has happened. Actually, worry lines scarcely ever furrow his innocent, unsullied face; everything comes easily to him. And this university student from the biology department, who stumbled across Darwinism at some point along the way, gets straight 'A's for every class, adding yet another 'Three Goods

Student' award to those he won a dozen years before in primary school and junior middle school. The pity of it is that he has never expressed a whisker of interest in insects, birds, fish or flowers neither then nor now. He has never been mad about or feverishly pursued any special interest, and it has certainly never occurred to him to aim for any kind of recognition. But he leads an agreeable life, and everyone has a good opinion of him. He's like an obedient rabbit: in order to get the diploma society demands he happily races between the designated white lines. I, on the other hand, am a stubborn tortoise. Sticking tenaciously to my own feelings and opinions, I slowly crawl forward from the starting line of quite another track.

Circumstances and habit have naturally brought us very close together. Our friends and elders all think that he couldn't be better as far as I'm concerned. Yes, he is, he really is a fine boy. We get along well with each other, and if you asked me to tell you what his faults are, I couldn't say for sure. I have reflected that life with him would be smooth; I wouldn't have to worry about him running off with anybody, neither need I be frightened he might take a big fall. But love should contain an element of the chase or else it falls short. I know, I was in love once, and so even though that first love, which aroused all my passion, was a mistake, I have tasted love, and it certainly wasn't like this! When I'm together with him, I often find half my attention wandering . . . he tells me sincerely that I have a driving disposition which pushes him on to make unremitting efforts. Huh! I'm not his supervisor, urging him on; it's me I'm whipping on, forcing myself to crawl further ahead. Nevertheless, it does make me feel as if I've grown up too fast. To me he gives the impression of utterly helpless strength; it's as if we weren't lovers but big sister and little brother! Every time I find myself under his respectful and totally trusting gaze, I experience a faint sensation of being helpless and alone, and feel sad that it is impossible for us to share any kind of tacit understanding of life's manifold experiences.

I looked out on the milling crowd through the window. Occasionally this thought will flash across my mind – supposing there is a potential close companion among the crowd of people passing me by, but we miss each other and go our separate ways. Would we never know of each other? You I came across quite by chance! But even then I missed you. Why? And if it hadn't been for that script I wrote! If I hadn't first of all dragged you off the bus? Then perhaps – oh! Perhaps the fact that we only got to know each other by coincidence presaged that in the end I would lose you.

It was a Saturday evening then, too, and just as crowded. Something was wrong with the middle door so I jumped out to fix it. At long last I managed to get it shut, but when I got to the front doors I discovered that there really were too many people, and I would have a hard time trying to squeeze back on.

Straightaway the boys on the bus set up a cry, 'Wait for the next bus! There's another one coming. Ticket sellers, show your tickets before you get off!'

I had to ignore them! Were I to give them a withering look, they would think they had impressed me and shout even more. Without a word I pushed aside the crowd of people pressing on to the bus, and grabbing hold of the last person to have got a foothold, his body still hanging out of the door, I pulled him off. I didn't so much as cast a glance at him, but merely heard him shout, 'I'm in a hurry! It's urgent!'

'Huh! Who isn't in a hurry to get home?' I threw back at him in a fit of annoyance brought on by anxiety and exhaustion. As I spoke, I had already taken his place and stood with my feet planted on either side of the door. Shouting 'Move along! Move along!' I put all my strength into getting on to the bus. It looked as if I would do it, but suddenly a much greater counterforce pushed me back off.

In that split second I caught sight of the person I had shoved off the bus. Thirty-odd and quite ordinary-looking, he glanced at me as he lit his cigarette. What did he think he was looking at! As I tried to squeeze back on to the bus for the second time, I heard his voice behind me saying, 'Here, let me help you push. Honestly, I do have some urgent business!'

'There's trouble enough without you adding to it!'

Gathering all my strength I made another assault on the door, using my arms, legs, hands, feet and my whole body . . . but that wretched woman in a woollen scarf turned herself around, blocking the way forward as if she was guarding the entrance. Her hair was in my eyes, but I couldn't free my hand to brush it away. The boys were still kicking up a merry racket while most of the passengers, sunk into an indifferent silence, seemed to be completely deaf. I couldn't move an inch! I felt a sudden rush of self-pity – I was only a girl after all – but, grunting with the effort, I kept up my desperate pushing and shoving with a grim determination. I had no time to weigh up the relative strengths of the crowd and myself, but I did know this much: one way or another I had to squeeze on to that bus as it couldn't wait around much longer!

All of a sudden someone started to shove on to the bus behind me. A violent force that brooked no opposition lifted me bodily up and forward. It was him! What stubborn determination! . . . I literally had no time to open my mouth, and was aware of nothing but a quick succession of battering ram-like assaults of tremendous strength. The folding doors quivered and then with a long, painful groan they finally closed.

The bus started up. I craned my neck a few times, but I couldn't catch a clear glimpse of his face. All I could see was a hand still clutching a lighted cigarette. I felt quite grateful towards him, as well as a little bit annoyed, but as usual I simply issued the curt order, 'Extinguish your cigarettes!'

And it was you! How could I have thought I might succeed?! Well, what do you think I ought to have done then? Pleaded in gentle tones? Sat down in the road and cried? . . . How I would love to come before you now with shrinking gentleness, even if I were just to gaze silently at you without uttering a word or moving a muscle! Were anything like that ever to happen again, however, I couldn't guarantee that my instincts would lead me to react in a more appropriate way.

That Saturday evening was both quite ordinary and very special. I remember every moment of it. . .

That evening I arrived late for the play reading. We were working overtime putting on more buses and so I didn't even have time to make a phone call. I could have asked for time off, but not many of my workmates knew I was studying creative writing, and I didn't want to make a big fuss about something that was still in the embryo stage. Even if I was to talk in only the vaguest terms, who knew what vivid details those sanctimonious wits might cook up in their heads, so there was no need to help them with embellishments.

Just as I got to the top of the creaky narrow wooden staircase, I heard a man's voice. I realized in an instant that he was reading my playscript, and was almost at the end.

I didn't go in immediately but stood alone by the door listening. The deep, vigorous voice was full of kindness, and immediately stirred me to the core. Maybe it was because I had fought by myself against failure, carefully mapping out my play only to cast it all awry, writing word after word only to tear up sheet after sheet. This thing which had troubled me for so many nights, issuing now from the lips of a stranger, suddenly gave me a whole new feeling and a satisfying sense of peace! I'd had a day of crowded buses which had left me sweaty and exhausted, I'd had nothing to eat, but everything was momentarily forgotten in the sound of that voice.

The voice stopped and I opened the door.

It was a large rehearsal room. Facing me was a row of huge peeling mirrors. There was a big circle of people sitting in the centre of the room. Judging by the sound of his voice, the man who had just been reading the script was sitting with his back to me, talking about something.

'I'll say it again, people must not arrive late for rehearsals! If you want to come and go as you please, then please leave now. This is art, not acting for your own private entertainment.'

I was taken aback by such a serious, peremptory tone. Quickly and quietly I tiptoed in from the edge of the room, busily putting together some apologetic words of explanation in my mind . . . when all of a sudden I halted, feeling the urge to turn round and rush out – just as I got to the mirrors I suddenly recognized him – how on earth was it possible?!

But he had already risen to his feet. Turning slightly, he put out his hand.

It was you! How could it have been you? The director? Oh no!

We shook hands and you introduced yourself. I most likely uttered some small politenesses, but I was in a complete daze and just stared blankly at you!

Strong and sturdy, broad-shouldered with a short, flat-top haircut and a full, round face. Capable men, good eaters who sleep well at night are often like that. Not at all surprisingly, you weren't a bit that kind! Sitting in the circle of graceful young ladies and handsome young men, you looked like a casual labourer or navvy. There was an earthenware pot in this collection of delicate, gold-edged painted porcelain! That was the comparison that struck me straight away. People who have nothing special about them are bound to get to know each other! As a rule I generally deal with any awkwardness by means of the weapon Ah Q types use to boost their courage, and so I simply would not bow my head, and instead carried on staring at you . . . and met your eyes. I don't know why, but all at once I was strongly drawn towards them. . . Your eyes certainly weren't particularly beautiful, but your level gaze had a quality of self-confidence and deterrent force about it. As you spoke, your eyes sparkled as if with amazement, while you sized me up with scepticism, and then you quickly gave a slight smile. The people around us hadn't discerned anything, or perhaps they thought it was just a sign of friendliness. But I felt the expression in your eyes contained a hint of humour and amusement, as if you had suddenly remembered some joke! To tell the truth, at the time I really didn't like that look you gave me, it was too cocky!

Whenever I was together with ordinary people, I always had to put on a tough front to conceal and protect my weakness, but quite by chance you had caught me in a tight corner the first time you saw me! I never should have minded what kind of figure I cut before you. I'm not a lifeless dummy standing exquisitely turned out, both hands raised, in some shop window arrangement! But I nevertheless felt a little annoyed.

Perhaps this feeling lasted only a fleeting moment, and then I felt we had been standing face to face for too long. I hastily withdrew my hand from your firm grasp and reached up to touch my face. I don't know whether I thought it was dirty or if I felt feverish, but straight afterwards all that came out of my mouth were the frank words, 'Please forget about it, next time I won't make things so difficult for you!'

'Thanks. But what if I don't buy a ticket next time?' he replied with a smile.

You and I looked at each other and laughed. The actors laughed too, but in fact they had no idea what about!

On first sight I had quite a good impression of Liu Jie who was to play the lead. She was shy and quiet, or might it not have been shallowness? My main character was shrewish, but she did have inner depth. And that was how I wanted her played. With total enthusiasm I pinned my hopes on Liu Jie. But when we started to analyse her role, she still just flashed her big, beautiful eyes and murmured a few inconsequential remarks. After hearing a few of her lines, I gave up hope! So that's what kind of young lady she was – hiding her inner pallidness behind a quiet and gentle reticence. The charm expressed by beautiful eyes outweighed the entire content of her inner self. But for the moment I kept quiet.

While you busied yourself establishing the roles, explaining the play to the actors and discussing the costumes and scenery with the art designers, I sat silently on one side, casually looking over the objects around me. Bits of scenery, doors and windows and all sorts of props lay at the side, an old-fashioned country oil lamp next to a duelling rapier, tables and chairs of all different styles but all equally out-dated . . . my initial excitement had passed, and little by little I calmed down, and moreover doubts began to creep into my mind. I had envisioned this play about the lives of young people today as a kind of tableau brimming with deep emotion. But to be performed by this amateur spare-time district theatre group, with these mediocre actors and under these conditions . . . perhaps when it was actually staged, the play would just be a pretentious, loud-mouthed little skit striking an attitude?! . . . there was a world of difference between what I wanted and the reality of what could be achieved. It's all too easy to set painstaking standards and a high asceticism for yourself, but you ought not to have even the slightest illusions about, or the least expectations of, the audience. Sometimes you are simply left helpless. . .

Just as this disturbing train of thought was set off in my mind, it seemed as if I had been given a tranquillizer as I quite unconsciously became aware of your strong, amiable voice.

Oh, so you were right in the middle of expounding the director's conception of the play! I turned my head and furtively observed you with keen attention. Soon, I felt an indescribable shock! How queer, just at that moment your unexceptional, ordinary face had undergone a change! A steadfast self-confidence, invisible yet tangible, and an upsurge of enthusiasm created an almost indiscernible change in the lines in your face, which projected a unique fascination. I caught the enthusiastic reaction in the eyes of the actors, and I too gradually became infected with it . . . was this the director's power? I have to admit your analysis of the play was correct, and in some places you had delved even deeper than I, the writer, and what you conveyed was even more stirring. But it wasn't only that. I dimly felt that for so long, so long I had been searching for, waiting for just such a person – absurd! What could I have been thinking of?! I knew next to nothing about you apart from your appearance, your job, your temperament. But judging from my intuition I seemed to know so much about you. . .

At last you turned and said to me, 'I really like this script, I've found it very moving. But there are just one or two places that need a few changes. It often happens that scripts don't quite tally with the demands of staging.'

Of course I wanted pointers, but I wanted even more to hear your opinion. But after a few words, I impatiently burst out with my ideas of what I had intended.

'What are you being so impatient for? Listen to what I have to say first, OK?'

I kept quiet for a while, but then I couldn't hold back the pressing differences in my thinking any longer . . . then I suddenly noticed that in your eyes clouded with deep thought there was a curious gleam of laughter. Only then did I realize how loud my voice sounded. The rehearsal room had already emptied, leaving just the two of us, but I was shouting as if addressing a busload of passengers.

We walked down the stairs one behind the other. You stopped under the light on a landing, and once again looked me over from top to toe.

'I never would have thought it! Your playscript is so fresh, so pleasing, and yet you're not like that at all!'

'What *am* I like then?' I thought you had finally come round to the way I was on the trolleybus, rough, coarse and incompetent.

'Ambitious. Not many people like that!'

These words far exceeded my expectations. I thought I should feel embarrassed, or take exception to such praise, but I simply couldn't keep back a desire to laugh.

'Just from looking at your script I would have imagined you to be quite a gentle, deep young lady, but in actual fact you've got a little bit of a man about you!'

He was a true director! And now he'd turned his character analysis on to me! I can recite a whole list of accepted feminine qualities: virtue, yieldingness, forbearance, gentleness, quietness, reserve . . . but your evaluation didn't upset me in the least, because in fact I would much rather be like I am. Your words coupled with all the new, stimulating events of that evening stirred me into an argumentative mood. I quickened my pace down several steps and came to a halt beside you, trying to marshal my woolly ideas into some semblance of order.

'In my view, society today makes much higher demands on women. What with family duties and work in society, we shoulder the same amount of the burden as men, or perhaps even more, which leaves us no option but to be as strong as men. Yet I've often felt it's a pity there are so many men lacking the manliness they ought by rights to possess.'

'Yes, it's not easy. . .' You didn't say what you thought of my ideas straight off, but dropped your head and began to rub your wrist which seemed to be swollen. I was going to ask you where you had banged it, but then you raised your head and leaning forward as if you were looking for something, you looked me up and down and said, 'Have you always been so self-confident and ambitious?'

Did I really appear so 'arrogant' in your eyes? Was I too open and direct? Or perhaps it was because of my habit of straight speaking and laughing with no attempt at concealment?

In actual fact, though, inwardly I was often full of hesitations and self-doubts, both before and when I met you.

But when I meet with failure, when I feel there is no more hope, I still keep calm. . .

I walked on slowly and aimlessly, and then on impulse found a bench in Ditan Park, where I sat wrapped in deep thought . . . that playscript had started off as a filmscript. I had failed, and it wasn't the first time. I really didn't understand, and there was no one to give me pointers, so I had to grope forward by myself, relying on my feelings. I hadn't counted on a victory . . . but the characters who had peopled my mind day and night were suddenly buried by defeat. My rich, colourful, passionate fantasy world that I had lived in body and soul suddenly shut its door, and for a while my heart felt bleak and empty.

The warm sunshine caressed my face and hands. It was a rare fine winter's day with a clear brightness and blueness to the sky, but I was oblivious to it all.

A young couple approached, the boy with his arm around the

girl's waist, and sat down on the bench opposite me. They were a few years younger than me, yet so bright and cheerful, and without a thought for who might be watching them. The girl laid her head against the boy's shoulder, and for a while he kept still, savouring this pleasure, but then he grew restive and raised his shoulder to shake her. As the rays of sunshine fell on her face, she languidly narrowed her eyes, and her lips moved almost imperceptibly as if she was saying something. The boy patted her smooth, pink cheeks, while the girl reached up to pinch his nose. Laughing and teasing, the pair jumped up to leave. Hand in hand, they ran off down a path leading off through the woods. . .

Watching their receding figures, I felt so envious! How could there have been joy and excitement in my pure and innocent first love, which had hardly begun before it was over? Even before I had a chance to mess around happily on the lawns, or let myself go and play chase in the sunshine, love vanished. And now, I have again let slip chances to enjoy so many brief, small pleasures, and wasted so much time when I could have been doing something real. It's as if I have a kind of semi-obscure sense of mission, towards all those of my generation, living or dead, walking, crawling, standing still, lying down . . . life has provided me with so many impressions, but what I am able to express is so shallow, so little. Maybe my complete helplessness and talent for writing have laid a yoke too heavy for me upon my shoulders. But if I were just to throw down my pen here and now, and become an uncomplicated simpleton, would I really be any happier? To tell the truth, whenever a sense of my own weakness and incompetence in everyday life or in my work comes over me, I long to shed a few tears on a trusted shoulder and release some of my pent-up bitterness. . .

But who can I rely on? A big boy once threw a stone at me when I was little. Frightened, I ran for my life, but then Daddy came! I immediately scrambled up on to his shoulders and his broad back seemed to me the safest, most solid shield in the world. Daddy is dead now, but even if he were still alive he wouldn't be able to help me out, nor understand the bitter loneliness deep within my heart. The reason is, he isn't of my generation! Li Ke is a good chap, but not for an instant someone I can depend on, he's far too frail!

So I have to count on my own strength in everything.

That's right, self-reliance!

This time it's just the same again.

I couldn't remain seated quietly on the bench any longer, and allow myself to get sentimental, or to go over it again and again. I know myself only too well. Whether I give up hope for three seconds, ten days, a fortnight, it's all the same: I still have to stand on my own two feet and carry on. Every day the buses have to keep on running, and I on the bus have to keep on shoving and pushing, have to keep on shouting. There's no choice in my job either. So that's why I have returned to my failed writings, and picked up where I left off, just like a mule returning to the whetstone to plod round and round again.

You valued my struggle, but still required me to fit in with feminine standards. But if it hadn't been for my arrogant, masculine spirit, how would I have got to know you, how would we have trodden the same path?

Perhaps in your eyes I remained the same from when we first met right up to our final parting. Yet you can never know how much was awakened in me during that brief time we were together. My memories of it are still so distinct. . .

At your desk in your little room, the desk where I sat only once, we went over my playscript, correcting and revising by the light of the table lamp.

Apart from our unbringing and personal histories, which couldn't have been more unalike, there must have been some areas within ourselves where we were identical, otherwise why were we always at loggerheads when we worked on anything together? You had your director's way of thinking, and I had my original ideas. Even though I wasn't familiar with the theatre, I didn't totally agree with your judgments. Once we reached a complete deadlock, when I flung down my pen and sat blankly at the desk while you paced up and down, silently smoking a cigarette.

Once, I'm not sure quite when, you acted out the script, declaiming and gesticulating, taking on all the parts yourself. As you acted, you made some changes in the characters' moves, while at the same time staying in control as the director. I both admired and was frightened by your agile mind. During your impromptu performance, your tiny little room, scene of conflict, was transformed into a magical place where one's imagination could run riot.

I was entranced. Little by little new ideas sprang up in my mind, and seizing my pen I noted them down on the script. . .

But however hard I tried I could not change anything in the female lead's several long soliloquies. They might have been rather long, but they would not have put across my ideas sufficiently had they been any shorter. They formed the core, the essence of the play, even you had to admit that. But you still kept telling me that when I wrote like that, the action was weak and only part of the artistic conception could be given expression.

Each of us stuck to our guns. Your elderly mother came in to see what the noise was about, and it seemed from her anxious expression that she thought we were about to start a war!

'I see that you're extremely stubborn.'

'Take a closer look – I'm your mirror!'

You and I stared solemnly at each other for a moment, but couldn't restrain our smiles.

'Where did you study directing?' To tell the truth, I inwardly admired you.

'A spare-time hobby! When I was at university . . . I never thought I would be doing what I am now!'

You suddenly let your fluttering hands fall, and stood stiffly, your eyes fixed on an oil painting on the wall. It was *The Ninth Wave* by Aivozowski, who focused on the ocean for his themes.

I didn't know what you were thinking. I went up to the bookcase. The moment I had entered the room I had noticed how many books you had, and I made up my mind to pick out a few worth leafing through. On closer examination they all turned out to be books like *Guide to the Oceans*, *Motive Power in Vessels*, *Nautical Astronomy*, *English for the Ocean-going Seaman* . . . Of course, there were also a few *Shipping Knowledge* magazines lying on the desk!

'So you like the sea, do you?'

'That was my major at college!'

I was flabbergasted! You went out to get some hot water while I tidied up the papers on the desk. Exactly what else was there in this confident, enthusiastic man? I was dying to know.

On the table was a copy of that week's broadcasting schedule. The top page was covered in red biro underlinings, all marking musical items. I would never have thought it. Just like me, you had found the same way to appreciate the classical music that one very rarely got the opportunity of hearing at a concert! As I pushed the newspaper to one side – perhaps it was feminine intuition – I caught sight of a girl's photo among the photographs and pictures under the desk's protective glass cover!

She was terribly pretty! Large dark eyes, and a quiet, gentle appearance. The only thing was that the photo was a very old one, and hadn't come out very clearly, which made her face lack depth and appear slightly pallid, while her eyes lacked lustre which gave her a faintly sympathetic look. Who was she? I knew you didn't have any sisters. . .

All of a sudden I felt extremely ill at ease as if I had rashly stumbled upon someone's private place . . . when I heard the sound of your footsteps outside the door, I hurriedly stuffed the photograph back under the glass and scattered over it the papers I had just tidied away, subconsciously hiding my 'crime', which in fact was no crime at all.

You sat down and picked up the playscript to set to work again, and then suddenly your face darkened. I stole a look – damn it! In my haste I had somehow slipped the photograph into the script.

'It's Mother's doing again!' You frowned, turned the photograph over and put it back in the right place.

Rather unsteadily, I quickly stuttered out an admission. 'It was me. Where . . . where does she work?'

'She's dead. She died a long time ago, during the Cultural Revolution. I tore this photo out of her student card.'

I'm sorry, really I am! It never occurred to me that I would unthinkingly bump against an old wound of yours that had never healed. And I never thought that you, the casual labourer or 'navvy', should have been a sailor!

Originally you were a graduate in navigation, but in the Cultural Revolution you were put in prison for political reasons. You made your living in all kinds of ways, but you could never go to sea. The policies changed, but the verdict continued to affect your chances and you still couldn't get proper work, so now you were rushing about here and there trying to find a solution. Not long ago you had read my script on a friend's recommendation. While you had been at university you had picked up skills in directing, and so had got this temporary job. You put it as simply as that.

'For someone who ought to be out pitting his strength against the sea to be directing a crowd of kids, while dreaming every evening of the sea in books and magazines – it's really rather laughable, don't you think?'

No, no! Not funny at all! I was silent for a long while. You sat in a dark corner behind the lamp so that all I could see of you was a stocky body, completely motionless as if carved out of stone. Yet I completely and utterly understood you. Even though we hadn't known each other for long. When the paths of two distantly separated people cross, that moment of chance has a certain inevitability about it. I understood you even though you had such a self-denigrating way of talking. I, too, never talked much about my problems to others, but rather made a light joke of them. Oh, but how could I compare myself with you! Now, in my spare time I could still gradually temper myself through my writing; but you, you yearned to practise your profession, but did not even get the chance to stand on a ship's deck!

I wanted so much to heave long, long sighs over your past, but I restrained myself. It was too shallow, I thought, to sympathize solely with sighs.

'Is there anything I can do to help? Even if it's only something very small!' All of a sudden I had this hope.

It was precisely during those two days that all the talk was of how Seiji Ozawa was coming on another trip to China. The boys were looking forward to getting another look at the unique way he carried himself, and quite by chance you came out with the remark that you would like to hear him conduct Beethoven's Ninth.

My day off happened to fall on the day they were selling tickets. I went out very early to queue up but came away empty-handed. I wasn't going to give up the idea so easily, and suddenly I remembered Li Ke, perhaps he could help – his uncle was in the philharmonic orchestra. I tried to call him up all day, and in the end I went round to find him. I rarely asked a favour of him, but whenever I did he always did everything he could to help out. But when he produced a ticket for the second performance he seemed to have more of an air of astonishment about him than usual. It suddenly dawned on me why: I wasn't behaving normally. I was like a young girl awakening to love for the first time who, spurred on by some nameless enthusiasm, is read to expend an ever-increasing amount of energy just to satisfy one simple desire. . . .

———

But Li Ke had only given me one ticket! Naturally he felt duty-bound to accompany me, even if he didn't care much for music.

I pedalled furiously over to your house. As I took out the ticket, I said casually, suppressing my panting breath, 'Oh, I've been already.' But inwardly I felt a slight twinge of regret.

A surprised smile came over your face, and I felt extremely pleased. But turning the ticket over to look at the date, you wrinkled your brow in regret – that evening you had a rehearsal. Then up came your mother and snatched the ticket out of your hands.

And so the well-intentioned Li Ke sat next to an unknown elderly lady. It might have been comical, but that ticket was really a sore point to me, although of course I couldn't say so!

So, to get a ticket for the final performance I had no alternative but to go and queue up.

At the door of the Red Pagoda Concert Hall I ran into you!

You stared fixedly at the one yuan note protruding from my fist and wordlessly looked me up and down. Under your scrutiny I, for the first time, tried to avoid your gaze as I feared your acute eyes would detect something I myself wasn't clear about which had just put forth its first shoot in my heart.

We wandered up and down the wide flight of steps amidst the stream of people going in one behind the other. Every time we bumped into each other we exchanged silent smiles. In your hand there was a two yuan note!

I smiled slightly to myself, not so as to attract the attention of the people trying to exchange tickets, but because of the secret you had just given away – each of us covering up and trying to explain things away.

An emaciated young woman with rimless glasses furtively tugged at me and took out two tickets. My luck was in after all!

When the theatre emptied we found the bus stop was very crowded.

'Let's walk to the next stop,' you suggested. I was obviously quite inured to crowded buses, but I nodded in agreement.

We walked along, exchanging comments about the concert, and then the conversation turned to the play we were rehearsing. As usual I talked non-stop, but my heart wasn't really in it.

'Could we walk a little slower?' you asked.

Oh, it hadn't occurred to me. I had ended up walking as fast as I usually did! In fact, I very much wanted to spend longer with you, and even secretly wished that the bus stops would be far apart. Actually, walking fast was just a habit! It wasn't just rushing to get to work on time, but because I was kept busy doing things here and there. Even my posture had changed. What hasty steps, I rushed busily towards the appointed place, with no thought as to how I looked, my chest and shoulders thrust forward. . . . Were you laughing at me again for being like a man? I consciously slowed my pace and quietly kept my lips together. But this careful attention made me feel rather strained.

'So quiet – what's up with you?'

'Nothing – I'm fine!'

'If I ever get to go to sea I'll be able to think back over this evening.'

'Why don't you just drop it all and go in for the arts? You really have the understanding it takes. Among all your complex qualities the main one perhaps is that you're practical. People like you, whose very appearance gives people that feeling – hey, don't get angry!' Once again I was talking too much in my impatience.

'I see! You've been observing me! – You're quite right, I do very much like the arts. The strength of feeling in art is itself a kind of happiness which encourages an enthusiasm and yearning for people, life and nature, even under the most extreme hardships. When I was escaping from the detention centre, all alone, covered in wounds from beatings, and running pellmell through the inky night, penetrating the gloom came the faint yellow glimmer of a lantern from a rustic hut in the wilderness. It seemed so soft and seductive, leading me, someone who had been cast out of normal life, to appreciate and understand that eminently ordinary little household's deeply moving qualities. Lying stretched out among the hills and valleys, completely exhausted after the most onerous hard labour, the wind blowing, floating clouds, the gently swaying grass at your side, the rolling swathes of forest, like ocean waves, could make you forget all your sorrows, blend in with the silence of nature, and let your spirit be at peace. . .'

We had passed the next stop, and neither of us had stopped. You talked, I listened – and that's how it was. We walked past stop after stop on the clean, freshly sprayed street.

'. . .but I want to do a practical kind of job, especially now.'

'You should be leading a comfortable, easy life at last, but you still want to go wandering on the seas?'

'Yes, I know. I'm at the age where I should settle down, but I still have a restless heart!'

'Maybe you're relying on your sixth sense. Have you heard the tolling of the bell beneath the sea?' I had developed an interest in *Shipping Knowledge* in the reading room.

'To be honest, whenever I go round to see any of my old classmates and look at their homes I'm full of admiration. In the street I caught sight of a dear little lad toddling along. I could have stood and watched him for a long time, but I know myself too well. While I was chasing a job I might have had a flash of regret that I had missed out on the joys of life, but in the face of life's selectiveness there lurks another constant deep discontent. I always think of those years of effort which still have brought me no closer to my ideal. China is just starting to develop ocean-going enter-prises, and there is a real chance that. . .'

I became absorbed in listening to you speak, drinking in your every word about the sea in the same way as the sea sucks in water to itself. I longed to know everything about you! But it seemed as if there was always more to hear, and that all I was left with was a vague impression. After a moment it was as if my thoughts escaped and quite irrationally turned to the perfect Li Ke . . . it was his disposition which had naturally set him on the smooth path through life; he would never be sucked into the whirlpools of disaster and difficulty. Birds have wings to fly high, but they cannot make any further progress along the evolutionary road from amphibians to primates. . .

You on the other hand would always be able to scramble to your feet wherever fate dumped you, and continue on your way. Just like an eel passing through streams and valleys which despite all the setbacks and detours, guided solely by its genetic programming, in the end reaches the ocean, sooner or later you too would be able to go to sea. . .

As I listened to you, I was yet not listening. I turned my head to steal a look at you. As I studied each fine line on your face, hoping in this way to be able to grasp more of your temperament and qualities, my powers of rational analysis vanished from my mind, leaving me in a blurred, dream-like state where I never wanted to take my eyes off your face, nor to think any longer, but just wanted to hear your voice, to lean just a little against your shoulder like this, and silently follow you onwards . . . sometimes I think how strange it was, yet also how annoying, for in my heart of hearts I longed simply to touch those firm, strong . . . could this all be really true?

'We won't be home before dawn if we keep on walking like this. Tired?'

I so much wanted to keep on walking like this, but suddenly I was tongue-tied.

As we crossed an intersection, a night truck tore past and I instinctively grabbed your arm, unintentionally touching your sore wrist on which you had stuck a plaster.

'What's this?'

'A souvenir of our first meeting. But it's nothing much!'

So you had banged it helping me to squeeze on to the bus! I carefully lifted your wrist to inspect the wound when suddenly I felt your concentrated gaze upon me.

'Why are you staring at me?'

'You're just like her in every way. . .'

'Her? What was she like?'

'Quiet and gentle, yet ambitious. She studied turbine design, and during our practical we were on the same ship . . . we never had the time to talk about anything much, but we did make a pact to devote our lives to the development of ocean-going shipping. . . One day on the college campus, she happened to cross my path. I very much wanted to hail her, perhaps I already had a premonition of disaster, but I was just too embarrassed at the time! She quietly walked by, right into a battle which had broken out between two rival factions, and a stray bullet went straight through her. . .'

'She was really ambitious, and yet quiet and gentle,' I repeated softly, taking all the sadness you felt as my personal sorrow.

'You're like her, but different too. I hope that your personality will change; there's absolutely no reason why you can't be strong, relying on your innate feminine qualities. . .' In that instant a look of deep tenderness appeared in your eyes, a look quite out of keeping with your temperament, and then it was quietly concealed along with something else. This was not merely sincere advice directed at me, I thought, but also regretfulness towards her. . .

My head was suddenly awhirl with thoughts, and I couldn't think of anything appropriate to say. The very last bus arrived, and I gave a shout, 'Quick! Run! See you at Wednesday's rehearsal!' I deliberately chose this discordant manner of leave-taking to conceal emotions I would reveal in the future. It was a habitual defence, yet it also turned out to be a pity; I hadn't had time to say anything to you!

After work I walked along the alley under the dim streetlamps on my way home. A cyclist came past me. In that instant I thought I recognized the profile. 'Have you come to see me then? Unfortunately I'm not in!' No, it wasn't a bit the same! In a flash my intuition suppressed all the conjectures which had sprung up in my mind. Even if the time we spent together was no more than one sweep of the clock's face, everything about you, inside and out, was fused within my heart. Even if it was the very image of your profile, if even an artist would be hard put to paint in the tiny differences, temperament alone would still be able to show a tremendous difference!

'What's the matter!' I scoffed at myself. 'He's tied up with rehearsals. What's more, he doesn't know where I live, much less what I'm thinking!' But I couldn't help thinking in spite of myself, 'If there really was such a thing as telepathy, it would be so much better!'

You couldn't have known that after the concert I had the constant hope that I would be able to see your thoughts, a hope that your eyes and my gaze would contain the same idea. One day, this shallow desire would linger no more. . .

Whenever I sit myself down in front of my desk, I find I cannot face pen and paper in peace. I still have a section of the novel to finish, but I can't write a word and my heart is ill at ease.

Without the sustenance of emotion life is dull and lonely; whenever I am suddenly swept by a perplexing feeling, it can lead to yet another different uneasiness! It really is so difficult to satisfy both parties. In front of Li Ke I am conscious of my own great strength, while my emotions will never be satisfied. I couldn't help being led along by him, I'm always thinking of him, and I want to improve myself as he hoped, to bring out that natural feeling of dependency that I myself have firmly suppressed. But what about that feeling of not wanting to pour out my woes to just anybody, what about my self-confident inner self, dragging itself forward step by step with such effort? It seemed I wasn't quite so tough at this moment. Nevertheless, when it came down to it I only had myself to rely on! This was the verdict on my life, which I was quite helpless to do anything about.

I turned on the radio, thinking to calm myself in the music. It was Beethoven again, the Concerto in F Major. Even without knowing the title it gives you the taste of spring, and at that moment this came over very arrestingly. I am no longer able to immerse myself in any of the concerto's superb movements. My mind is always elsewhere, always thinking of you, wishing that you could be there listening too. . .

It is as if I am walking along by the side of a clear stream with the upside-down reflections of a line of newly green poplars. At every step, caught in the fork of each tree there appears a dazzling sun, following me! You are constantly before my eyes, and you never go away! . . . Oh, wherever I go, there you are!

'You shouldn't make useless sacrifices out of emotion! Perhaps my feelings have got out of hand. And what is it really? A soap bubble of emotion blown up by myself! A soap bubble reflecting all the colours of the rainbow from a little bit of sunshine. . .' I was analysing myself with cold reason, striving to ridicule myself. But it was no use whatsoever! People are queer; a single idea can mysteriously change the whole tenor of their lives. . .

Here I was, worried about you, and you had not an inkling of my concern but were rehearsing other people for the play! Liu Jie, the female lead, and the other girls – how jealous I was of them, how I envied their position! They were listening to you speak, watching you attentively, being inspired by you – good heavens! What was I thinking of!?

These thoughts that I had no way of explaining by kept nagging at me! In my heart I dared to confess it: I had fallen in love with you!

How did you actually feel about me? Did you like me or not? I had no way of knowing. Despite the fact that men have their separate outlooks on the world, I know that generally speaking they all have more or less the same evaluations and requirements as to what a woman should be like. And that includes you. As for me, someone who led you to say that I had a bit of a man about me, there was no way I was what people liked! How strange! I used to understand this, but on the contrary felt proud of my abruptness and ability to stand on my own two feet. But now, I just have a slight feeling of despair. How did I come to give you that impression?! I was lost in deep thought . . . I have to admit that some elements of my personality were involved. I have to cope with the pressure of society and protect myself against people spying on my private affairs out of curiosity or jealousy, and so I am obliged to put on a mask, even a masculine one. But putting this aside, would I be able to change into someone a little more lovable? Yes, I would. I wasn't born like that. . . . It appears I really have changed in some ways. But when? My memory pours forth numerous trivial and unrelated incidents. . .

Carrying water along the steep, rugged mountain path, a little would splash out on to the yellow earth where it would soak in, leaving not a trace behind.

Shouldering a huge pile of gunnysacks weighing over a hundred catties, I had to gather all my strength, grit my teeth and move upwards step by step.

What should have been the most enjoyable ten years of my life were spent in blue clothes coming and going in constant displacement, quietly worrying about my brain which was gradually filling of its own accord, and deliberately shrugging my shoulders.

The first time I overcame a timid feeling at the bottom of my heart and used the phrase 'your mother's', it was in imitation of the authentic sound. Afterwards I could swear like a trooper when I got annoyed, and even when I was cheerful curses would come rolling off my tongue.

When Daddy was sent down to the countryside all Mum could do was cry. I had to comfort her, do something about Daddy and carry on my life at the same time! Where could I find a job then? I pleaded, sent gifts, negotiated . . . frailty and bashfulness are necessary weaknesses in the perfect feminine nature, but I resolutely stripped them away and went out to deal with all comers!

He went back to the city first, and our love was over. Should I have cursed him? Should I have longed to die? That would have been idiotic! Alone, I struggled to bury my emotions, and coolly considered what to do next.

That's how it was. On the emotional side, I dared not whole-heartedly throw myself into love any more; it could vanish in an instant, which would be too tragic for words! At work on the buses, I had to put in as much effort as the men; and in everything I undertook there was no one at all I could rely on. All I had was my failure staring me in the face as I started over again. As for politics, as for the path I have taken through life, with all the choices open to me I relied solely on my own decisions. Is this totally my own fault?! God, if there is one, made me a woman, but this society has demanded that I be like a man! So often I preferred to deliberately conceal my feminine traits just to survive, just to keep on going. And so, quite unconsciously, I've become like this! Isn't it possible that I'm not the only one? If she was still alive, if she had been through those years, what would she have turned out like? Even if she still remained quiet and gentle, what about her thoughts, her inner self?

I have thought about it a lot. If I came out with these ideas nobody would believe I was just a twenty-seven-year-old girl. Life had forced us to wake up to ourselves, to look deep into ourselves. It's not that I've grown up too quickly, more as though I'm old for my years. This kind of wisdom is in itself also a kind of grief.

But now I had you in my life, and everything was different. I wanted to change myself completely for you, and be a proper woman!

Just before falling asleep, I glanced once again at the calendar on the wall; Wednesday: I mustn't ever be a single minute late again!

It seemed as if every passenger taking a ticket from my hand, every passenger getting on and off the bus beside me was looking at the pale green nylon gauze scarf I was wearing at my throat! I hadn't put it on too early in the season had I? I constantly glanced at the people around with uncertainty, hoping to find others wearing the same thing. Being dressed differently and attracting the stares of others is quite the most embarrassing thing, even if it was only a gauze scarf! Before leaving home I had looked over myself in the mirror, but then it hadn't seemed overdone . . . Oh, these little, trivial, unspoken thoughts!

When we handed over to the next shift, I went to the clinic at the central bus station.

'Turpentine oil? Where does it hurt?' As Wang, the doctor who also acted as nurse, stared closely at me, she kept a watchful eye on her entire property, a little medical chest with the lacquer peeling off. I actually had to take off my stocking to show her before she would unlock the chest. She took out a clean, empty bottle, and carefully half-filled it with turpentine oil.

'Here you are, careful! Your foot. . .'

I'd already disappeared!

I skipped up the creaking stairs two at a time. As I reached the last few steps, I heard laughter and voices issuing from the rehearsal room, and I immediately slowed my pace to one step at a time. The actors were already all present, and the room was buzzing animatedly. Some were practising their dialogues, others sat, their chins on their hands, in silent concentration as they went over their lines in their heads, while to the side a few more were chatting about something with lots of laughter. I didn't so much see as rather intuitively feel that you hadn't arrived!

I went over to the desk in the corner and gently placed the medicine in the drawer before sitting down to wait. Some of the cast came over and told me excitedly that they were going to hold a dance after the performance on the first night.

'I'll trample all over everybody's feet! I really can't dance!' I hastily explained.

'I'll teach you!' said an actor enthusiastically, swaying his body from side to side as he half-sat on the edge of the desk.

Smiling, I thanked him, all the while worried that the bottle of turpentine oil would topple over, and I could feel my face taking on a most peculiar expression!

'You're not likely to get a turn!' said Liu Jie with a quiet smile. 'It ought to be the director who invites the writer! You both argued and fought so much to put on this play; it really wasn't worth it.'

'Were we really that terrible?' I heaved a sigh, not without some regret. I put on an even more bashful air, and bobbing my head and holding out the corners of an imaginary long skirt, I said to the actor in a delicate voice, 'I beg your pardon, sir!'

At this unexpected performance, the actors were all highly amused. Unable to keep up the facade, I too broke into laughter.

Through our laughter I suddenly heard the sound of footsteps coming up the stairs! The sound was virtually indiscernible, but I did hear it. Nearer and nearer it came, that measure, that weight – I could tell it was you! Instinctively I stopped laughing straightaway and fixed both eyes on the door. To take a phrase you used when talking to the cast about stagecraft, it was as if I too had taken note of my own behaviour, consciously or unconsciously, to make sure it wasn't too exaggerated.

You walked in rapidly, taking off your padded coat as you apologized to everybody. I had the feeling that your apology seemed imbued with a barely concealed happiness . . . I carefully noted your every movement, but in fact you hadn't even seen me, which might have been because I was sitting in the corner. You gave the whole cast some brief instructions, and then sat down on a chair in the centre of the room. The spotlights came up.

I sat back in the shadows and watched the performance, but all the time I was aware of your slightest movement. There were still a few small changes to be made, but the adjustments all went very smoothly. My own feelings followed the leading lady's passion as it moved on and changed, while at the same time one question went round and round in my head: what had made you late?

When the play got to the part with my favourite lines, there was a bang from the table and Liu Jie stopped. You pointed out that she wasn't putting enough feeling into it, and that she had got the rhythm wrong.

Liu Jie's big eyes took on a sparkle of pathos, and she pouted aggrievedly, 'That's what's down in the script, I honestly. . .'

You thought deeply for a moment and then said, 'Right, we'll change it then.' You called all the on-stage actors together and conferred for a while, then the play carried on from where it had left off.

What? You really had changed it! The characters' moves and positions had all altered, and lots of lines had been cut. The play had become totally different in this section; this wasn't at all what I had intended. Here I was, sitting in the room, and no one had even bothered to consult me! I couldn't help being annoyed. I had it all thought out: this time I would keep my temper and sit politely at the side, and I would speak slowly, moderately and with reserve, even if it was my feelings that were being discussed. But the words were on the tip of my tongue, and however hard I tried to hold them back I simply couldn't restrain myself, and let out a loud sigh.

You turned your head and glanced at me, and then jumped out of your chair and came over.

'Oh, so you're here. I'm so sorry, I didn't have time to compare notes with you. Anyway, what do you think of the changes?'

I just wanted to make a few points and then stop, but you argued for your views, so I had no alternative but to keep on talking. Actually I had no intention of arguing non-stop with you, but I had no choice in the matter, my characters just had to stay as they were! Once I got started, I became excited, I talked faster and faster, and my voice grew gradually louder. I talked and talked and then suddenly it occurred to me that if I carried on arguing, you would again think me stubborn and pushy – your opinion of me could never change! I suddenly stopped talking. After a while I sat down wordlessly and looked at you. You were saying something, but I didn't catch a word of it as I was too busy controlling my temper.

'. . . is that all right then?' I suddenly heard you say.

'What?'

'To make these changes!'

'I . . . no, it's not!' I burst out, thumping the table. The actors all stopped and turned to look at me, whispering among themselves.

'You're being unreasonably stubborn!' you said hurriedly in a low voice, while at the same time patting my hand which lay on the table in a soothing manner. Then you turned to the cast and said, 'Who told you to stop? Carry on, carry on!'

Damn it! Was even the tacit understanding and trust between us to be regarded as unconditional surrender on my part?

'Don't you give me that crap!'

Instantly you stopped and withdrew your hand. Turning as if to leave, you said, 'Cool down a bit. In a while we'll have another little chat about it.' Then you left me on one side to simmer down.

As soon as the rehearsal was over, you tore off down the stairs to take a phone call which had been awaiting you for some time. The

actors left one after the other, and I remained sitting motionless.
You came back upstairs, grabbed your coat and walked over to me.

'Still angry?' you asked gently.

I thought of explaining the ideas inside me, but I still felt
annoyed and upset, and suddenly came out with, 'Why the hell do
you always mess things up for me?'

You misunderstood me! You looked at me for a while, probably
feeling that I was stubbornly rejecting other people's opinions, and
thought I was always right. You sighed. 'I'm sorry but I've got
something urgent to do. When I have time, I'll go over this with
you in detail.' You finished speaking, turned and left!

Leaving me all alone.

It was then that I got really furious – with myself. What the hell
did I think I was doing! For a fantasy world such as this, for a few
lines, a few details of a character who didn't even exist, I had
damaged my own image. At that moment I really envied girls like
Liu Jie who were so quiet and gentle, whether by instinct or design!
If all along I had been gentle, refined, and soft-spoken, and hadn't
stubbornly clung on to such a trifle, but instead had smiled at you
and let it drop . . . but I could never get to be like that. Oh God, I
never meant to quarrel with you! . . . I believed that my tough
masculine stance was just a cover; I had no idea it had gone so deep
into my character that even if I wanted to I couldn't shake it off! I
really gave up hope for myself!

Suddenly I discovered that I was standing in front of the row of
slightly distorting mirrors. I looked absolutely furious! With my
hands thrust into my pockets, boots speckled with dust, and the top
button undone on my cotton padded jacket, my pale green gauze
scarf hardly merited a second glance. As if to mock me, this careful
attention to detail just looked pitiful against my ridiculous, coarse
actions! Suddenly snatching the gauze scarf, I pulled it off and
stuffed it into my coat pocket.

Opening the drawer, I took out my gloves to get ready to leave,
when I caught sight of the little bottle of turpentine oil! I felt like
throwing it out of the window but instead I put it in my pocket.

Of course, I knew very well that most of the changes you had
proposed were quite right! This was on the first night just after the
curtains had swept open. I was standing by the exit with one eye on

the living action unfolding on stage, and one eye on the audience reaction. In the blending of the emotions running between those on stage and in the audience, I was deeply moved by strengths in my play that I hadn't even known existed. I wanted straightaway to admit to you that some of my original ideas had been wrong, but you were kept constantly busy backstage . . . I would make sure I talked to you at the dance afterwards, I secretly resolved. I had even quietly tried out the waltz a few times, so as to be able to dance with you. . .

The response to the play far exceeded my wildest expectations. I was kept busy accepting everybody's congratulations while at the same time anxiously waiting for you to hurry up and come, yet hoping that we would have a little time together in quietness! Liu Jie was completely surrounded; her performance had turned out much, much better than I had ever expected. People called on her to talk about her characterization of the role, but she put on a bashful air and simply smiled without saying anything. When she saw she really could not get out of it, she collared me and pushed me forward, saying, 'The credit for my performance should go to the director. He filled me with inspiration so often, and told me to study the writer. He said that she was just this kind of woman with an overly masculine temperament.'

As I stood in front of the crowd, in an instant I was struck dumb by this comment! I would never have thought it; so that's how you regarded me! You used me as a demonstration model, with not the slightest inkling of my inner self. Everyone gave me friendly smiles of approval, and so all I could do was smile back although my heart was in misery!

The music struck up. Several people came up one after the other to ask me to dance, but I politely declined. I sat alone behind a pillar, and it was as if I was far removed from the happiness of this trivial achievement. I was bored, and I suddenly felt very tired and wanted only to close my eyes and listen to the music.

'Would you like to dance?' somebody asked me in a low voice.

'I have a headache,' I excused myself automatically.

But straightaway I knew it was you who had sat down next to me. Even though I was deeply hurt, I instinctively started to feel jittery and couldn't help seizing on the topic I had earlier thought out while watching the play. 'The play. . .' I stopped. Originally I had intended to admit my defeat but now I didn't want to. All right, let you think I was stubborn and unreasonable, for that's just what I was in your eyes.

'Why is it that every time we meet we talk about the play! Let's talk about something else for a change! We still haven't had any time to talk about anything!'

How come your voice was so different? I lifted my head.

You were smiling slightly, but the smile seemed to contain a touch of melancholy. For a moment I was left speechless, and could only gaze at you in acquiescence. Then I met your eyes. They didn't seem as acute, as confident as usual, but were clouded and abstracted, and in the middle of this entire hall brimming with joy, in the midst of so many exuberant, smiling faces flashing past, for an instant I suddenly felt that there was something holding our gazes together. . . . I felt it must go beyond the limits of my control, and I would soon have to admit defeat and hastily shift my gaze.

'Shall we have a dance?' you asked again.

I stood up automatically and placed my hand on your shoulder. But just at that moment, the music stopped. Suddenly your comment came back to me, and that courageous streak in my nature which makes me unwilling to bow my head lightly, came rushing to the fore. Deliberately cynical, I said, 'It looks as if we're not destined for each other.' I was smiling but my heart was quivering.

Quite by chance, Li Ke came rushing over to me, dodging between the dancers.

'This is my boyfriend!' I said vindictively by way of introduction.

The music started up again, with a Cuban number, 'La Paloma'. I hastily grabbed Li Ke's shoulder as if to escape, and said of my own accord, 'Let's dance.' Not caring whether or not he'd heard me, and keeping to the beat, I literally dragged him into the centre of the dance floor.

'I'm the one supposed to be doing the leading,' Li Ke couldn't help reminding me. At every turn I looked across his shoulder and through the dancing couples to see you standing next to the pillar . . . at every turn I saw you . . .

Li Ke looked at me with that limpid, devoted gaze of his, and suddenly blushed and muttered, 'You're really fine . . . I'm, I'm very fond of you!'

Oh, it's quite awful! None of the people I like are fond of me, and those who are I can't stand!

Liu Jie and her partner went by, and still dancing she twisted her head to ask me, 'Will you be seeing him off then?'

'Seeing who off?' I asked, mystified.

'Our director!' She kept on dancing, now drawing closer, now moving away. '. . . He's going to sea . . . taking the 5.30 train to Guangzhou tomorrow morning . . . don't play the innocent, as if you didn't know!'

Instantaneously I relaxed my hold on Li Ke's shoulder, and stood in the middle of the dance hall. You had already vanished from beside the pillar!

Pushing and shoving my way through the happy crowd, I tore over to the pillar, colliding with people, stepping on toes and having mine stepped on, desperately searching in every corner, but you were nowhere to be found!

The dancing couples were like shadows as they noiselessly swept by in slow motion. There was just the sound of a lone voice, deep and melancholy, very close by and yet seemingly far away, singing:

> The day I left the home I love
> My heart was filled with sorrow. . .
> Oh let me follow you like a dove,
> Soaring free across the sea. . .

I don't know how it was I got to your house. The small room was darkly lit, and I could just make out your parents. They said there were a lot of people you wanted to say goodbye to, and they were afraid you wouldn't be home until very late.

'Is there anything I can do for you? Or is there something you'd like me to give to him?' inquired your mother kindly. She looked at me expectantly. I couldn't stand there for ever, but what did I have to give him? I hadn't brought anything with me, I hadn't had time to think of anything! My hand unwittingly went to my jacket pocket and closed on a small medicine bottle. I hastily pulled it out.

The bottle was empty! At some point the turpentine oil had leaked out all over my pocket and soaked away. . .

I had reached that stop again! There you were, standing quite still under the blue and yellow checked bus stop sign! Your broad and stocky body, that dull red flicker of light at the side of your mouth as you dragged on your cigarette; that view of you under the street lamp . . . for a split second the illusion was so clear, so intense!. . . Under the sign there was a mass of people surging down the pavement, crowding their way along, but you were never among them!

I jumped down from the bus, and was the last to get back on after everyone else.

What part of the wide, wide world were you drifting through at that very moment? On that undulating, restless ocean, leaping with myriad golden points of light, what were you doing now? As you stood by the side, looking up at the twinkling night sky, what were you thinking of?

The shadows and bright lights, the tide of people and the stream of cars rushed forward to meet me and then passed. The bursts of ringing from the bicycle bells sounded like a sprightly nocturne suddenly breaking out from the continuous deep trumpeting of the traffic, and then fading into the distance. All around me was bustle and hubbub, but I felt lonely.

The snow was melting. Everyone's shoulders and hair glittered with fine pearly drops. The bus was filled with a fresh, clear dampness, and the breath of spring silently permeated everything. A sudden gush of emotion rose and filled my heart.

How I longed to see you again. To see your eyes, your instantly unforgettable gaze. I wished that memory could be suspended so that I would always retain that comfort and strength achieved for a fleeting moment . . . but it seemed forever separated off by a mist, and the harder I tried to hold on to it, the more indistinct it became. Your eyes, your gaze; it seemed that just as I was about to see them clearly, they suddenly receded into the distance, far far away . . .

I bumped into you, and then lost you! Where did I miss you? I've racked my brains and searched every inch of my memory, I've looked back over every scene in our brief period of contact:

. . . the noise and excitement of the dance
. . . the conflict at the rehearsal
. . . the long slow walk after the concert
. . . your desk, that I only sat at once

. . . the creaking stairs

. . . the side of the folding doors of the bus which wouldn't close because of the press . . .

Oh, what has kept us apart is not endless high mountains and deep rivers, not the boundless ocean, but myself!

The bus came to a halt. I went forward again.

The same as ever, she forcefully pushed her way forward through the passengers, her lips mechanically repeating, 'Passengers boarding the bus, buy tickets! Give up your seats to mothers with children. The next stop will be . . .'

But at the bottom of her heart, she is crying out in quite a different tone out of lonely repentance:

'. . . Forgive me . . .'

Translated by Angela Knox

BECAUSE I'M THIRTY
AND UNMARRIED

XU NAIJIAN

NOW MY HOUSEHOLD registration has been fixed, those solicitous for my welfare have all urged me to waste no more time but 'a-wooing go, hey ho!' But would I be able to adapt myself to that happy rhythm? Even so, I have still joined the ring of dancers treading measure in search of a partner.

A strange man sat opposite me. He was sizing me up until I began to feel most uncomfortable. The devil alone knows why it entered my mind to do so, but I tossed back some stray strands of hair from my forehead, revealing all my wrinkles, as if as on a lighted screen.

I finally worked up the courage to look back at him, just as he was sneaking a look at his watch. Oh, it was as clear as lightning that I'd been rejected. Life's penalty for latecomers is always disappointment.

What rubbish we talked, what a load of rubbish. The half hour was over, we were now shaking hands as briefly as possible and politely saying, 'See you some time.' What we ought to have said in fact was, 'I won't be seeing you again.'

'You just don't put yourself forward. You're simply behaving like a fifteen- or sixteen-year-old kid,' scolded my cousin on the way home. She had arranged the introduction.

It was late autumn in the park, and a layer of dead leaves covered the ground. They crackled under foot with the crisp sound of ripping silk.

'You simply don't try, you don't put yourself forward . . .'

'In this respect a thirty-year-old spinster is much the same as a fifteen- or sixteen-year-old girl. One is still unconscious of her charms while the other is all too aware hers have vanished.'

'Not at all, your problem is that you don't act civilized.'

'I'm just a country girl who's been tucked away in the countryside for ten years.' I gave a bitter laugh. 'But even the country girl has her own little inner world, how else would I have got through up to now?'

'You have a point there, what kind of a life did you have? Who could imagine that you never had a sweetheart from the time you were twenty!'

Five years my junior, my cousin was just waiting for a place to live before getting married. Her clothes, her expression were modern enough to be just right, and she had plenty of self-appreciation. As we went down the street, she attracted everybody's gaze.

She stopped in front of a shop window to check her reflection, tossed back her long permed curls and repositioned the gleaming blue hairslide.

'I can't believe no one has ever captured your heart.' My cousin leaned forward and fixed me with a crafty stare.

All I could do was heave a sigh.

'Come on, you've experienced some kind of tender feeling, haven't you?' she probed. 'A confusing, muddled sort of happiness where you have only to think of the person and your heart brims over with contentment, where you long to see him, and think up all sorts of excuses. . . . But at least you must have got letters from someone, eh?'

'I seem to remember I did, but it was a long time ago.'

'Then you. . .'

'I . . . didn't write back.'

'Heavens above! You have simply no feminine sensibilities at all!'

'I'm all too aware of what it was like to be an educated youth! That's all there is to it!' Suddenly my anger boiled up. The unhappiness I had just been trying so hard to express, all at once welled up in a flood which rushed to my lips and mind.

One by one I had put aside things in my life, thinking that when I returned to the city I would arrange them, yes, I would deal with them then. . . . The lake's surface was a mass of dancing golden motes . . . but this was how life had disposed of me. . .

'Toffee threads spun out of thin air, toffee threads spun out of thin air. . .' At the park entrance, a young man was shouting this as he did conjuring tricks. How absurd! The phrase has stuck in my heart just like sticky toffee threads.

We waited an irritatingly long time for the bus to come. My cousin seized the opportunity to try and sort me out.

'Don't wear this grey jacket next time, you look like a wolf's grandmother in it! Get yourself a pair of low-heeled shoes, straighten up a little, and show a little more spirit. . .' When she was little, she had begged me to braid her hair and tie it with a butterfly bow. Now our positions had been reversed. In this one respect, it was as if I had flown up to heaven and whiled away ten years, returning to earth only to find I had grown younger. 'What kind of bra is this you're wearing, so big and ungainly? Get yourself one of those bras from Xinjiekou. They're a nice shape – made in Guangzhou. You're so out of date. We can pick out you returnees at a glance, you know.'

'If you didn't have us at the bottom to compare with, you wouldn't appear so fashionable.'

'So I ought to be grateful. How about another introduction, what do you think?'

'No, I don't want to go through all that again.'

'Oh, don't take it all so seriously, that's no way to "a-wooing go, heo ho!" If at first you don't succeed, try and try again. In other words, this is not the time to be sitting around twiddling your thumbs, you've got to learn how to catch your man.'

'You devil!'

She pulled a face. 'All right, here's my phone number, 22078. When you finally come round, phone me. But don't hang about too long, there aren't that many catches knocking about. I'm not kidding.'

The bus arrived.

'A Min, well, how did you get on then?' Unable to contain her curiosity any longer, Mum finally asked me about 'that business'.

'Not so well. It's over.'

'Already? So quickly?'

I didn't reply. I leaned back against the quilt, and reached for my book to hide behind.

Mum stood looking at me for a while and then left the room. It's not easy being the mother of a thirty-year-old unmarried girl.

I was sick to death of it all! Obsessed scientists and librarians, modern-day gifted scholars and beautiful ladies all of them! People didn't have such melodramatic love affairs in real life.

But really the book wasn't so bad, as the writer had in fact captured the feeling of being disappointed in love. However, I don't believe that's the most wounding unhappiness of all. I mean, after all, if you fall in love you're bound to get splattered with emotion. The real tragedy lies in someone whose heart is like a dried-up well. How did I reach this point? From the age of twenty I have spent my time talking ceaselessly of transferring back to the city, heaving sigh after sigh. My youth was like the dim, faint light of the paraffin lamp by which we used to stitch the cloth soles of our shoes. Just what did those ten years leave me with?

I know an excellent little poem which really touches me to the heart – I can even recite it from memory:

'. . . Only three young men out of a hundred
Returned home to their families – ah yes.
Time is a healer of wounds,
Anger and indignation can be stilled,
But for those husbandless girls of the 40s,
What can be done?
Just twenty at the time of Liberation,
They are in their fifties today,
And left to secretly envy
The children and grandchildren of others. . . .'

War, that was war, but to our surprise we who have never been touched by war find ourselves in the same position!

'A Min, why don't we go out and see a film, eh?' suggested Mum softly. She must have come in at some point, and had sat down at the head of the bed. She wanted to cheer me up but actually there was no need.

———

'Is there anything good on? I can always guess the endings!'

There was a silence.

Mum looked as if she wasn't going to give up that easily. 'Well, how about a cruise up the Yangtze River then?'

I was on the point of saying I wasn't interested when I noticed a fleeting look of sadness cross Mum's face, so I swallowed my words. Poor Mum, your concern alone isn't going to fill me with contentment; I need something different.

I heaved myself off the bed and tidied my hair. 'Shall we go then?'

Mum nodded. What a joke. Neither of us actually wanted to go on this pleasure trip. Mum thought it was to cheer me up, but for my part it was in fact to cheer her up.

What kind of a pleasure boat was that, crammed full of people and not even a railing to lean over! The deck was so packed with passengers that not even a breath of fresh air could penetrate . . . just like the slave ships in the films.

We ought never to have come.

As the boat passed under a big bridge, a steam locomotive thundered past overhead making the whole structure tremble. Even though the cars and buses streaming across it were pretty antiquated, the bridge had a slightly modern look about it . . . like a man in his great-grandmother's side-buttoning mandarin jacket.

How odd. There were so many courting couples on board but when we got off at the Ten Li Dyke at Xuanwu Lake they didn't stroll off but stood pressed together like sardines.

Good heavens, that couple had even brought binoculars along with them and were making a great show of looking through them.

What's that woman shouting for? She's smiling so winningly you would think there were only the two of them on board.

Look at that woman's perm in front! With all those tight little curls perhaps it's called the chrysanthemum style. Rather vulgar, she looks like a poodle.

So stupid! What has all this got to do with me?

We really ought not to have come.

I went back into the cabin and sat down next to Mum, taking the tangerine she held out to me. When I was little a tangerine could keep me happy for a whole hour, so what about this bagful now?

The muffled purr of the turbine engine sounded as if it issued from the stomach of a cow. It was a sound I was very familiar with as every year I had chugged up to the town and then back to the countryside in just such a small shorthaul steamer. People said it was a tiring journey but I had loved it. For so many years the only bright spots had been those days spent en route to somewhere. It seemed as if Fate had smiled on me then.

To this day I still don't know who he was. He sat opposite me with a blank look in his eyes as if he was gazing at someone in the far distance. He fell into conversation with me very naturally, starting with a few scattered remarks. As his gaze gradually cleared and focused, it turned out that he was open-minded with a highly original point of view, and some of what he said immediately permeated through to the minutest fibres of my being. I should have given him my name and address as I could see from the expression in his eyes that he knew my worth, that he understood people. As I became aware of this it seemed as if the whole world had warmed to me. Fate so seldom recommended anyone to me, but . . . I let the ball thus tossed to me slip through my fingers. What made me think of life's first and highest aim at that particular moment? What a disaster!

Is my situation today a punishment for lacking courage in my life, or is it a penalty for my serious attitude towards life?

'The Skater's Waltz'. Those people over there are craning their necks again, Swallow Rock is coming up ahead, but what is there to see – it's just a bare rock.

We really should never have come. My mother and I both exchanged looks.

I must be developing an interest in children, although when I was first assigned to the factory nursery I did make a bit of a fuss.

Little Meizi was once again crouching in the corner by herself away from all the fun. Just looking at this yellowish-haired kid, whose family had moved back from the countryside, gave me an indescribable feeling. Her little wizened face made her appear much older than the fresh-faced little girls who had grown up in the city, and she still enjoyed playing 'chopping pigs' swill' with a bit of broken tile, wandering here and there about the courtyard.

I went over to the corner. Little Meizi was talking to herself in her northern Jiangsu provincial quack. 'There, there, dolly, don't cry. Mummy'll give you some milk.' She'd found an old eye-dropper to serve as her feeding bottle, but where was the dolly? Was it that handkerchief mouse? A sorry little dolly indeed!

I squatted down and put my arm around her. 'Little Meizi, Auntie'll find you a big dolly, a real dolly to play with.'

'Will you really?' Smiling, she clambered up me monkey-style.

We had a beautiful big Western-style doll in the nursery, but it was usually kept locked away in a glass cabinet and only came out for the children to play with if we had visitors.

When she saw me unlocking the cabinet Little Meizi's eyes became like saucers and she even began to skip.

Ah, if a Western-style doll could coax her into such happiness, then what would it take to coax me? I'd already been coaxed by getting my transfer back to the city – not bad – and at the time I'd probably been as overjoyed as Little Meizi was with the big doll, but this kind of sop to happiness doesn't keep you happy for long.

Obliquely opposite stood the factory canteen, and the children would all rush over there whenever they had free time. I too made my way over to the canteen.

What a wonderful smell! What were those little devils doing lining up in front of the deep-fryer? Laughing and joking, the ruddy-faced cook was tapping their heads one after the other as one by one he collected the steamed buns each child had brought and tossed them into the deep-fryer. Turning back, he pulled a funny face, calling, 'Keep back! Keep back!'

All at once the deep-fryer began to sizzle and spit. 'Ooh! Aah! The little steamboats are going! The little steamboats are going!' cried out the children in an excited chorus.

It's hardly surprising I've begun to love them! As I entered, the little devils as one whipped their newly fried buns behind their backs and trooped out one after the other.

'Xiao Guo! Come and sit down here for a while and give us a hand with the vegetables.' These cooks never missed a chance to play a trick on someone, perhaps they needed something to help them digest all that good food they got to eat.

'Where would I find the time?'

'Come on, just for five minutes?'

I couldn't get out of it and had to sit down.

'Soon be getting a fiancé, then, eh, Xiao Guo?' asked an old woman who was busy stripping vegetables, edging forwards. I must be imagining things! It looks as if everyone has the right to make inquiries about a thirty-year-old spinster!

One of the cooks was putting the buns into the steamer. 'Two, four, six, eight – ' He counted them in pairs, and when he got to the end he picked up the last remaining bun and deliberately raising his voice said, 'Oh no! How come this one's all on its lonesome?' Snatching up a bit of dough he rolled out a bun and added it to the steamer. 'That makes it up to a pair!'

The kitchen workers burst into laughter.

I rose. 'This is sheer "cursing baldpates in front of a monk".'

'Only joking, don't take it so seriously. But in all fairness, Xiao Guo, you shouldn't hang about too long, eh? It's one thing for a man to be getting on, but for a woman – well, you have to try a bit harder, and then even harder. . .'

'Much obliged to you for your concern – but I'm the last act!'

Behind my back came the languid sound of the old vegetable stripper's voice, 'Old chives, a mouthful of grass; old aubergines, all seeds and nothing else; old kidney beans, two layers of shell. . .'

I was turning into an object of discussion. Why was I acting so sensitive, as if I'd peeled off a skin? If they wanted to talk, well, let them.

The canteen was buzzing. Today's topic under discussion was 'America's Singles', an article from the weekly digest of foreign news items.

I didn't want to sit with people I knew, they might very well come out with such wisecracks as 'Oh, Xiao Guo, so you're doing it the American way, are you?'

With my helping of cabbage and braised meat, I went to sit down opposite two girls who evidently were out-of-towners here on business.

'I don't like the set-up of the family today,' said the intelligent-looking one, spitting out a few bones. 'Things need to loosen up a little, otherwise a woman may as well forget about getting anything much done!' She tossed back her short hair animatedly.

'Forget that! What about independent space? Do you have any place just for you yourself? No, none, we're all so closely stuck together. Your sort of dreams are not about to be realized; first we need to deal with the dreams of people who only want eight square metres of floorspace so they can get married.'

'If that's the case, then people just aren't going to stand for it. It only needs someone to raise the banner of the single life and I for one would respond to the call for sure.'

'Puritan!'

'Quite the reverse. I don't want my love to wither away in eight square metres.'

They finished their meal and left the table joking together.

It was a clear autumn day, and the sunlight glistened on the soup bowls.

For quite a while I sat pondering over what they had said, but in the end of course I drew a blank and returned to square one. I didn't need to expend all my energies on my work, nor would I ever manage to be as free and easy as that woman. All I wanted was to lead an ordinary sort of life. It had been a real battle arranging my transfer back to the city; it hadn't been at all easy to pull off. I'd come back, and quite honestly I was exhausted. How nice it would be just to lean against a dependable shoulder and rest. But whose shoulder?

I hadn't even got to the door when I heard Mum chatting to someone inside.

Tian Lan, that's who it was! My old companion! To get our transfer back to the city we had walked over seventy *li* together and had collapsed with fatigue at the door of the county office which dealt with educated youth. It looked as if once again we were sharing a common fate.

'How's it going – found a husband then?' Nowadays it seemed as natural to ask that as it had in the past been to ask if someone had managed to get a transfer to the city.

'What do you mean, found a husband? More like I've reached my final resting place.' She was clearly in very low spirits.

As a rule we don't get together when we're in good spirits but only when we're feeling down. So once again it's just like when we were in the countryside together in that we go over our shared problems endlessly with a fine-toothed comb. The subject has changed, but our sighs are just as deep and heartfelt.

Our youth had been a complete and utter waste.

We talked on and on. All of a sudden Tian Lan became heated, just like that time after a meeting of educated youth when in a flash she had woken up to the realization that it was no good sitting around and sighing; if we wanted to get transferred back to the city we would have to do our own running about, pushing and grabbing.

'Xiao Guo, from the look of it this business of getting a boyfriend is pretty much the same as getting a transfer back to the city. We have to get people to help us, launch an attack. Fate has been tough enough on us already so what is there to get embarrassed about?'

'To be sure, we've got nothing to lose, so why worry about losing face?'

'No more giving up!' Tian Lan's eyes glittered with the challenge. Gazing at me she suddenly smiled. 'Still as countrified as ever, I see. Look at that great big bare space!' She pointed at my forehead, bereft of any fringe.

'You can hardly talk!'

'All right then. Off we go right this minute – to the hairdresser's.'

'Oh, not right now. Another time.'

'What do you mean "another time"? Just how many more times do you think you've got left? We've said we're going so let's go. . .'

Sitting under the permanent waver, I began to feel uncomfortable and awkward once again. At the age I should have been dressing up I hadn't, and it made me feel strange to be doing it now that my youth was drawing to a close.

What was the matter with this mirror? Was I really so ugly? The soapy water had soaked into my skin enlarging the pores and giving me a coarse appearance, while the wrinkles on my forehead stood out as if etched in silk thread. Wretched mirror!

I closed my eyes.

The two male hairdressers were having a lot of fun. Without stopping what they were doing they were jabbering away nineteen to the dozen. Did they have dates waiting for them?

'You've really got it together all of a sudden – got enough photographs of pretty girls in your hand to make up a pack of cards!'

Raucous laughter.

'Now its the turn for that gang of girls to get nervous. When they come round to present themselves, I have to size them up.'

The heat from the hairdryer was positively broiling.

Quacking laughter.

What a torture having to spend so much time getting your hair permed!

When I opened my eyes and glared at myself in the mirror, I smiled bitterly.

'You can't escape from the pressure of public opinion. It's terrifying.' As we came out of the hairdresser's, Tian Lan pulled a sorry face. 'The penalty for being choosy has come down on us. We're not in a good position and every extra year means a drop in our standards. We can't delay any longer. I wish you every success.'

'Keep some for yourself.'

We parted company.

I walked blankly down the street. How annoying, these bustling crowds of people! Where did they spring from?

This little side-street seems quiet enough, but it's too narrow.

Why have they left their door wide open? People going by can see right in. A big bed, a dining-table. . .

They've even got the stove in there. Actually, that's not a bad idea; bedroom-cum-dining-room-cum-kitchen, all three rolled into one.

The character for 'happiness' was stuck on the windowpane. Newly-weds. Fine, a new life was to begin in that little room.

I made my way over to a public telephone kiosk. What was my cousin's telephone number again? Oh yes, 22078.

An advertisement stuck on the shopfront opposite me read 'Clearance of Old Stock – Once Only Cut-Price Sale'.

22078. . . . .

'Clearance of Old Stock – Once Only Cut-Price Sale'.

22078. . . . .

Translated by Angela Knox

BIOGRAPHICAL NOTES
ON THE AUTHORS

BING XIN

I was born in 1900 in Fuzhou, Fujian Province. We moved to Shanghai the following year, and later I followed my family to Yantai, Shandong Province. My formative years were thus spent on the coast, and the sea became my great love, as shown in my earlier works. In 1913 my family moved once again, to Beijing, and the following year I entered a missionary girls' middle school, Bridgeman Academy. Graduating in 1918, I then enrolled at the Union Women's College where I studied science. At the outbreak of the May 4th Movement in 1919 I was secretary of the Students Union at my college, and wrote several articles to publicize the movement. My propagandist activities soon began to tell on the results of my science studies, and I had to switch to the literature department. By this time my college had already merged with Yanjing University.

I graduated in 1922, and managed to win a scholarship to study English literature at Wellesley College in the United States.

I completed my studies in 1926 and returned to China, where I taught at Yanjing University and the Women's Institute of Literature and Science at Qinghua University. My works published at this time included *Superman*, a collection of short stories, two collections of poetry entitled *Stars* and *Water in Spring* as well as a prose collection called *For Young Readers*. In 1931 the Beixin Book Publishers brought out *The Complete Works of Bing Xin*. Other published selections of my work included *The Past* and *The Girl Dong're*. During the War of Resistance Against Japanese Aggression I wrote a book called *About Women* under the pen-name A Gentleman. Following the end of the war, in 1946, I went to Japan. Between 1949 and 1950 I attended Tokyo University, where I took courses in the New Chinese Literature.

After returning to China in 1951, I wrote *After the Return* and other works, and a new life began for me. Fiction and prose collections of my works such as *A Selection of the Prose and Fiction of Bing Xin*, *After the Return*, *We Have Waked Up the Spring*, *In Praise of Flowering Cherry*,

Gleanings, A Small Orange Lamp were published by the People's Literature Publishing House, the Beijing People's Publishing House, and the Tianjin Hundred Flowers Publishing House.

In 1960, at the Third Session of the Congress on Literature and Art, I was elected a council member of the Chinese Writers' Association. I was selected as delegate to the Chinese People's Political Consultative Conference in 1978, and became Vice-Chairman of the Writers and Artists Association at the Fourth Session of the Congress on Literature and Art in 1979.

After the fall of the Gang of Four, *For Young Readers – Third Batch of Letters* began to appear in the magazine Children's World.

Apart from my creative writing, I have also translated *The Gardener Gitanjali* by Rabindranath Tagore in addition to his short stories, *The Prophet* by the Syrian writer Kahlil Gibran, and the King of Nepal's *Mahadra's Poems*. My own works have been translated into Japanese, English, French, German and several other languages.

YU RU

My original name was Qian Yuru, and I was born in Hangzhou, Zhejiang Province. At the outbreak of the War of Resistance Against Japan, I left my home town as an orphan and wandered through a number of places until I reached Chongqing. In 1938 I entered No. 1 Art Training School as a probationary student, and by 1939 had written my first short story, entitled *The Ganges*, which received a third class Young Women's Literary Award. Later I became the librarian at the Chongqing Film Studio. During this time I joined the number of progressive writers and artists in Chongqing and was given an introduction to the journal the *Literary and Art Front (Wenyi Zhendi)*, the editor-in-chief of which was Mao Dun. I got work there as an assistant editor, and began to study creative writing by myself. I wrote a middle-length short story called *Faraway Love*, followed by a short story entitled *Dream of an Eagle*. I returned to Shanghai in 1946 and found work at the *New People's Evening (Xinmin Wanbao)*. At the end of the following year I had to leave Shanghai for Hongkong, where I was a reporter for *Hua Shang Bao* and wrote a number of columns and features under the pen-name Ru Ru. In 1949 I moved to the *South China Daily (Nanfang Ribao)* where I was not only a reporter but also the deputy director of the art section. At that time I was mainly writing features and reporting on literature. Then in 1957 I transferred to the Guangdong Branch of the Chinese Writer's Association, where I engaged in writing again. In addition I went down to Xinhui County to experience life more deeply, working as assistant secretary to the commune. I published three collections of children's literature and a collection of raportages.

The past two years have seen the publication of *Longing for Mangos* and other raportages, prose pieces and short stories, as well as another collection of children's literature entitled *When We Were Young*.

RU ZHIJUAN

I was born in Shanghai in 1925 on the thirteenth day of the ninth lunar month, and from a very early age helped my grandmother eke out a living by taking in handwork. My family was in straitened circumstances, so I didn't start school until I was eleven, when I was enrolled in the Shanghai Puzhi, Private Primary School. After graduating from junior middle school, I went in 1943 to teach at the Yihe Primary School, a private school in Shanghai, for six months. That winter I followed my elder brother in joining the New Fourth Army, and joined the Modern Drama Troupe of the Battle Front in the Jiangsu Military Region as an actress. In 1947 I wrote the lyric for *We Fight Best When We March Our Hardest*, for which I won a second-class literary and artistic creativity award in the military region. My first short story *He Dong-liang and Jin Feng* appeared in the Shanghai paper *Wen Hui Bao* in 1950, and the play I wrote the following year, *The Soldier Without a Rifle*, received second prize in the literary and artistic creating awards from the Nanjing Military Region in 1955. In July 1955 I left the army and went to work for the Shanghai Writers' Association as editor of *Literature and Art Monthly*. That same year I joined the Chinese Writers' Association and subsequently was elected as the council member of the Association Shanghai Branch. 1957 saw the publication of my novel *Story Before Dawn*, which depicted the lives and struggles of youngsters, while in March 1958 the journel *Yan He River* published the short story *Lilies* which extolled the flesh-and-blood ties between the people and army. My first collection of short stories appeared in 1959; entitled *The Tall White Poplar*, it contained ten short stories and five feature stories. I began to devote my whole time to creative writing in 1960, and two years later the second collection of short stories *The Quiet Maternity Hospital* came out. The large majority of the stories in these two volumes were about the lives of women during various different periods, and the changes in their ways of thinking and feeling. At present I am a member of the editorial committee for Shanghai Literature. After the fall of the 'gang of four' I wrote a number of short stories, such as *The Path Through the Grassland* and *The Story out of Sequence*.

DING LING

Born Jiang Bingzhi or Ding Bingzhi in 1904 in Linli, Hunan Province, Ding Ling began to write in 1927. Soon she was publishing short stories and editing literary magazines. Having joined the League of Left-wing Writers in 1931, she joined the Communist Party in 1932 and became Party Secretary of the League of Left-wing Writers the following year. In 1933 her novel *Mother* appeared and she was imprisoned in Shanghai by the Kuomintang. Three years later she was released, thanks to Party efforts.

Throughout the next decade she combined her literary work with political activities. The time she spent living among the workers, peasants and soldiers and working with a land-reform project culminated in the publication of *The Sun Shines over the Sanggan River*, a widely translated, prize-winning novel.

Ding Ling held several important literary-political posts after the founding of the People's Republic of China in 1949 and published essays, prose collections, and short stories. In 1957, however, she was labelled a Rightist and her works were banned. She was forced to do manual farm labour for twelve years and was jailed during five of the 'cultural revolution' years. Nevertheless, she continued to write.

After her rehabilitation in 1978, she resumed her position as a leading Chinese writer. Her previously banned works have been republished, and a new novel and many new short stories have appeared.

In March 1986, Ding Ling, respected writer and revolutionary, passed away, deeply mourned by many.

ZHANG KANGKANG

I was born in Hangzhou in the early 1950s, just at the outbreak of the Korean War. When I was a year old my parents started to call me Kangkang, to distinguish me from the thousands of other little girls all born at the same time and named Kangmei, or 'Resist America'. Or it might well have been to commemorate the War of Resistance Against Japan, when their friendship and love had flowered during the joint struggle to decide the destiny of the nation and its people. But in any case, this peculiar name often reminds me of a number of things worth remembering.

I remained in Hangzhou as a schoolgirl until I was nineteen. From an early age I had been reared in the literary atmosphere of our home, and at school I came under the direction of my teachers, so by the time I was in the fifth year of primary school, I had published my first article, entitled *Studying to be Little Doctors*, in the Shanghai children's paper, *Literature and Art*. The first attempts strengthened my resolve to become a writer. I graduated from Hangzhou Number One Junior Middle School in 1966. Three years later my love and enthusiasm for creative writing led me to volunteer to sign up to go to Northeast Wasteland. There I stayed on a farm for the next eight years, during which time I was as a farm labourer, a brickyard labourer, a correspondent, a reporter for the propaganda section, and as a writer for the performing arts propaganda team. Conditions then were extremely difficult, and many was the time I did my writing on the edge of the *kang* or on my knees. My first story 'Lantern' was published in *Liberation Daily* in Shanghai in October 1972. The next years a prose *Chief of the Great Forest* and a short story entitled *Faun* appeared in *Wenhui Bao*, while in 1975 *The Boundary Line*, a long story about the life of educated youth and developments of the countryside, was put out by the Shanghai People's Publishing House. The following year the same press published a prose collection entitled *On the Great Land of Xiyang*, containing my piece *Lin Yiye, the Youth*, which appeared in English in the 1977 edition of *Chinese Literature*. Between 1977 and 1979 I spent two years studying in the Playwriting Department of the Cultural Bureau's College of Performing Arts in Heilongjiang Province. After 1979 my prose piece *Listening to the Waves on the Shores of Lake Xingkai, Ink Draught Lotus, Who Sends Letters Through the Clouds* and short stories *The Right to Love, Is He a Hero?* and *Summer, The Distance Chimes of the Clock* and *Pale Mist at Dawn* were published variously in *Northern Literature, Harbin Literature*, and *People's Daily*, battlefield supplement, as well as *Harvest October* and other periodicals. In 1975 I became a member of the Writer's Association of Heilongjiang Province and devoted myself to full-time creative writing.

DING NING

Ding Ning was born in 1924 into a poor family living in a small country town in Wendeng County, Shandong Province. As a child, she only completed primary school, but after leaving school she continued to study on her own, reading works of classical literature and poetry, as well as the 'new literature' which emerged from the May 4th Movement. She took on revolutionary work in 1938 and studied in a wartime middle school and at Kang Da (Military and Political Academy for Anti-Japanese Aggression). During the War of Resistance Against Japan she worked as an actress and artistic director in several theatrical troupes in Donghai District, East Shandong, and in the East Shandong Children's Theatrical Troupe.

During the war years, she produced prose and fiction, as well as a number of lyrics and skits. At that time she wrote under the pen-name Zi Ding and Ah Ning. Following the fall of the 'gang of four', Ding Ning was transferred to the Policy Research Office of the Ministry of Culture. Recently she has been writing prose works, and *The Poetic Soul of Youyan* and *An Ox for the Young* are among those which have already been published.

ZHANG XINXIN

I was born in 1953 after a difficult birth and was optimistically given the name Xinxin, which means Bitter Joy. My mother was a graduate of the Chinese Department of Beijing University while my father had had two years of schooling in a private village school before joining the revolution. Despite this he could write. However, from kindergarten all through school, whenever anyone asked me, 'What are you going to be when you grow up?' I never replied. It was only if my father ever happened to say to me, 'Whatever you do, don't become a writer when you grow up; it's too arduous,' that I would immediately retort, 'You mean if something is difficult you shouldn't do it? I *am* going to write!' I thought I would wait until I'd finished university and then see, but just after I had finished primary school, the 'cultural revolution' came along. I joined a production and construction corps in Heilongjiang where I worked as a farm labourer, and then went to Hunan as a soldier. There I became seriously ill for a while, and it was then that I began to study by myself. After I was demobilized I returned to Beijing, where I became a hospital nurse for a few years. In 1979 I was accepted into the Directing Department of the Central Drama Institute.

My short stories *In a Still Ward, One Quiet Night, How Did I Miss You?, Lodged in My Memory, Between Two Hearts,* and others; the middle-length short stories *On the Same Horizon* and *One Person's Secret* as well as reportage and a filmscript *To Your Health!* have appeared successively in *Beijing Literature, Harvest* and *Monthly Literary Miscellany*.

Writing is an arduous task. Studying at the same time as writing is even more arduous and contradictory, but I enjoy it. Perhaps this explains the riddle of my name.

XU NAIJIAN

I was born into an educated family of Nanjing in 1953. After only a year of secondary school I ran into the 'cultural revolution'. I graduated from junior middle school in 1968 and the next spring I left the middle school attached to the Nanjing Normal School to join a farm on the coast north of Jiangsu Province, which at that time was in army hands. There were close on ten thousand educated youths at the farm, together with farmworkers and a sizeable proportion of peasants, known as 'team leaders', who had been brought in to expand the farm. In the nine years I spent there, I took on a number of jobs such as farm labourer, commune accountant and secretary, primary school teacher, and so on. In 1978 I passed the entrance exam for the Chinese Department of Nanjing Normal College. I started my creative writing in 1979. My generation grew up in a disaster-ridden ten years. Bitter reality and a nightmarish kind of life forced us to face things squarely and to do some painful and serious thinking. Whenever we pick up our pens it is not so much to write as to spew out, to rid ourselves of last night's leftovers.

In the past two years a few of my short stories have been published, including *Poplar and Cypress Pollution, Because I'm Thirty and Unmarried, Big Xiangzi, The Knight, Little Smarty and Nimble,* and *Train No 52! Train No 52!*

FURTHER
READING

Seven contemporary women writers, transl. by Gladys Yang, Peking, Panda Books, 1982

Prize-winning stories from China 1978-9, Peking, Foreign Languages Press, 1981

Ding Ling, *The sun shines over the Sanggari River*, Peking, Foreign Languages Press, 1984

Ding Ling, *Miss Sophie's diary and other stories*, Peking, Panda Books, 1985

Yang Mo, *Song of Youth*, Peking, Foreign Languages Press, 1964

Many other stories can be found in the quarterly journal *Chinese Literature*, Peking, Foreign Languages Press.

Hsiao Hung, *The Field of life and death* and *Tales of Hulan River*, transl. H. Goldblatt, Indiana University Press, 1979

Dai Houying, *Stones of the wall*, transl. F. Wood, London, Michael Joseph, 1985

Zhang Xinxin, *Chinese lives*, London, Macmillan 1987

Zhang Jie, *Leaden Wings*, London, Virago 1987.